Music *summons* the savage beast...

Skilled Chicago surgeon Ethan Roddick abandoned his wolf heritage—and elitist parents—when heartbreak tore his world apart. He swore never to let love sink its fangs into him again, but when a meaningful family commitment lures him home to Stoke Ridge, his determination is tested by Gabriel Mendoza, a sexy human with soulful dark eyes and the voice of a bourbon-soaked angel.

Pressured by his parents to mate—to a suitable shifter, of course, and preferably a female—Ethan is instead drawn to the sassy singer whose heat seems destined to heal the rift between his two halves. As passions rise, so too do tensions, and anyone who's not a predator becomes, by default, *prey*.

Can these fated mates fight old clan prejudices and find their future together?

His Healing Heart

Gray Vale Pack

Book Three

Copyright © 2023 Evie Riley

Second Edition

ISBN: 978-1-77357-691-6

Naughty Nights Press LLC

Cover Art By Willsin Rowe

HIS HEALING HEART

GRAY VALE PACK

BOOK THREE

EVIE RILEY

CHAPTER ONE

Ethan

I TIED OFF the final suture on Maureen Brady's chest. Hinchcliffe, the chief surgeon at Mercy Hospital, simply shook his head.

"You're some kind of freak, Roddick. I've never seen a surgeon work so fast."

"If I worked at top speed, you wouldn't see me."

The theater was always cool, but it suddenly went cold. I was accustomed to that, and more than fine with it. These people were my equals only on paper. Not a one of them—not even Hinchcliffe—had one-tenth of my skill. It was one thing—perhaps the only thing—I could thank my wolf senses for.

"A little humility wouldn't go astray, Roddick."

I pulled off my gloves and pushed open the theater door. "Why, I'm simply following your own directive on efficiency, Doctor Hinchcliffe. What was the wording you used again? Oh, yes... if you don't need it, don't use it."

"And you know very well I'm specifically talking about surgery, Roddick. The faster we finish, the smaller the risk to the patient."

"I choose to apply it in life as well." I tossed the wadded-up latex into the bin behind me, without even a glance over my shoulder. "It keeps me from getting bored by conversations like this one."

As I shouldered through the theater door, I suppressed the smirk that tried to climb onto my mouth. I had a reputation as a cocky bastard, and I'd worked with all my usual attention to detail in order to cultivate it. Nobody ever got past that arrogant veneer unless I wanted them to.

Of course, mouthing off to the chief like that was sure to come back and bite me. A risk, for sure, but a calculated one. In the end, it barely mattered. I could bite back just as hard.

Harder, even.

For a moment, I held my breath, centering myself. Bears might be the ones who hibernate, but I'd done my level best to send my wolf into permanent sleep. Even so, the beast stirred within me, baring its teeth, scenting the air. I leaned against the wall, working hard to think human thoughts, pulling my emotions into check.

For months now, even the slightest sense of passion had called to the animal. Today, it was the elation of a perfect surgery, blending with the buzz of rebellion.

Neither of those could compare to the rush of blood frenzy, or the scent of an available mate, of course. But I'd starved my beast for years now, and clearly it was prepared to take whatever crumbs it could get. In the past few months, my wolf had begun to lash out with a fierce hunger.

Hopefully, that activity was nothing more than its death throes. Only when I'd finally closed down the fiend within could I think about opening my heart to another. Until then, I had to stand strong, and always on my own two feet. Never on four.

All scrubbed down again, I pushed my way into the corridor. Just as I reached the door to his office, Nurse Patrick came bustling up.

"Doctor Roddick."

"Tim."

"You had a phone call while you were in surgery. A Kiera Larson."

Tim held the note out to me, and I frowned but didn't take it. "It's been years. I'm sure it can wait. I have dinner reservations at Dominic's." A burst of guilt hit me for a moment. I'd never actively ignored my cousin Kiera. I'd just let life get in the way.

"She said it was urgent."

For my cousin to call me at all was a huge step, so I had no doubt it truly was urgent in her mind. But it was almost certainly about my parents, so as far as I was concerned, whatever the problem was could wait a while. And then it could go to hell.

Nurse Patrick pushed the note into my hand, cutting through my internal argument. I sighed and curled my top lip, as if the paper had come straight from the dump. "Okay. Thanks, Tim."

"Yes, Doctor Roddick." The man had already turned and headed back to the reception area. Such was my rapport with the staff.

I closed my office door and dropped

heavily into the plush leather of my reclining chair, moaning with muted pleasure as the padding embraced my body. Soft and accommodating, and eager to both take on my heat and mold to my form. My interaction with my chair was as close as I'd allow myself to come to another relationship.

At least until I found a cure.

For a moment, I crushed my eyelids together.

How had I so easily led myself back down that path, to the singular seed of all my pain?

The chief trigger that had led to me pushing away everyone and everything before they could even begin to matter to me.

I tugged in a breath, filling myself with cool air and holding it in for as long as I could. When I shot it back out, I let my pain go with it. The note felt inordinately heavy in my hand as I lifted it.

All it held was Kiera's name and phone number. If it had been anyone else from Stoke Ridge, I'd have tossed the note in the garbage. That place had scarred me like nothing else. Both in childhood and as an adult.

But Kiera had been like an older sister during my difficult early years. Her folks had shielded me from my own parents, and their unmasked shame at my... trouble. If not for the Larsons, I felt certain I'd never have made it out of adolescence.

With all that weighing on me, I pursed my lips and punched my cousin's number into my desk phone. She answered on the second ring.

"Kiera Larson Designs."

"Hey, Killa."

"Ethan! I seriously never thought you'd call back."

"Well, I didn't. I just put in the number for Dial-A-Ho and here we are."

"Har-de-har, scrotum-face."

"Answering your own phone these days?"

"My assistant is taking care of some, uh... urgent fact-finding research for me. At the patisserie."

"Uh-huh." I couldn't prevent the smile from curling its way over my mouth. I'd come to believe everything in my life was fine. That I didn't need anyone.

In only ten seconds, Kiera had undermined that very foundation. "I never thought I'd say this, Killa, but I actually miss you."

"Yeah, if that's meant to be sweet talk, then you probably should stick to insults."

"Noted. Now, what's so damn urgent that you're forcing me to be somewhat sociable?"

"This weekend. Back home."

"You must be joking. You know I swore I'd never go back."

"Things are different back there, now. You know we merged with Gray Vale?"

"Did you?" I no longer felt any sense of kinship with fucking Stoke Ridge. It did surprise me they'd blended with a pack that was supposed to be the enemy, though.

"We did. It's working really well. You'd be surprised."

"I'd be surprised if I ever saw the place again."

"Well, before you make any decisions, you need to know one thing. It's my parents' thirtieth anniversary. They specifically requested the presence of their favorite bun-from-another-oven."

I rested my head against my palm. "You know I'm one of those doctor thingies, right? That I can't just slice someone open and ask them to wait until Monday?"

"Oh, come on. Are you telling you're the only one in the whole hospital—in the whole city—who's allowed to play with cutty whatsits and stitchin' doohickeys?"

Using my work as a shield was such a clean—some might say surgical—way to avoid going back to hell. But the truth was, I had two weeks' leave organized, starting on Friday, and had no plans beyond holing up in my penthouse and glaring down at the city below me.

Chicago was about as far from Gray Vale as you could get. At least, in spirit. For me, it was the perfect antidote to the passions of nature.

I'd removed myself from the wilderness, yet the wilderness still had a hold on me. To go back would be to tempt my wolf out of its coma, and that was too much to contemplate.

Kiera interrupted my thoughts as if she could read them. "Please, Ethan. I know you have your issues with... y'know, everything there. But this is my parents. That has to mean something, even to someone like you."

"Like me?"

"Yeah. A bigshot asshole."

"Thanks for noticing. And yeah, it does matter. You know it does."

Her sigh came through the phone almost as a physical entity. "Honestly, buddy, it won't be nearly as bad as you think."

"You don't know how bad I think it'll be."

"I know you think all eyes will be on you. That everyone will talk about little Nimroddick and how he's become mister fancy-pants with his high-falutin' new life."

"I wouldn't have put it like that, but yes, that's how I think it will be."

Kiera scoffed down the line. "Please. Nobody will even notice you."

"Then what's the point of me going?"

"Because we built a fifteen-foot-tall rose gold throne with flashing neon lights on it for you. Duh."

"Yeah, you're right. Nobody will notice

me at all."

Kiera's cackle hadn't changed in five years. "Well, of course, you're completely free to refuse this invitation. To spit in my face. To leave a burning paper bag of doody on the doorstep of my heart."

"Don't think I won't."

"But of course... there will be a follow up call."

"Do your worst."

"From my mom."

"Oh."

"Uh-huh."

I took a fortifying breath, then opened my diary and picked up my gold-plated fountain pen. "So, what time are you expecting me?"

CHAPTER TWO

Gabriel

I JUGGLED THE two coffees and the paper bag of sinful goodies as I walked back to my desk. I couldn't help but smile as I watched my boss hang up the phone and punch the air.

Passing Kiera one cup, I sipped at my own. "Good news, boss?"

"Great news, Gabes. Wonderful."

"New client? Big job?"

"Not actually anything to do with work, no."

"Oh, you're getting married! And you want me to sing at your wedding. This is so sudden."

Kiera crossed her arms and rolled her eyes. "That kind of nonsense would require a living, breathing, devastatingly sexy male person, wouldn't it? Have you seen any of those around here?"

"Apart from me, you mean?" I did a quick and—hopefully—graceful pirouette on the spot.

"Dude, if you batted for my team, I'd have fired you months ago so I could ride your fine ass into the sunset."

"Fair point," I said, and sighed heavily. "But to answer your question, no. I haven't seen a hot and available guy since... I dunno. The Bronze Age?"

"Damn. Because just talking about it has made me hungry for one right now."

I clapped my hands sharply. "Your news, loopy lady. Tell me."

"Oh, right. No, I mean it won't really mean anything to you. It's a family thing."

"I love family things." I bit into my tongue, trying to suppress thoughts of my late parents.

"Well, this is extended family. My cousin Ethan, the cardio-thoracic surgeon over in Chicago. He's been the, uh... black sheep of the family for a while, but I just talked him into attending my parents' anniversary party."

I guessed that was somehow significant, but it kind of flew over my head. I doodled on the pad in front of me, picturing her cousin as a distinguished but balding man. Maybe stocky, with a porn star mustache. "Oh. I guess that is good news. I'm happy for you."

"Oh, hey." Kiera walked over and sat on the corner of my desk. There was a twinkle in her eye that only ever showed when she had some evil plan running through her head. "You got me thinking, though, Gabes. How is your singing going?"

"What does that—"

"Stick with me here. I will, eventually, have a point. You still sing? You weren't just fooling?"

"Part time, yeah. Down at the Crazy Rabbit. Jazz and blues standards."

"How's that working out?"

"I love it. If I couldn't sing, I think I'd die."

"You're such a drama queen. And the

pay?"

I doodled a little more, adding extra randomness. "Well, let's just say it's lucky I do it for love. I sing for tips. And last week I only made enough to split a pack of cigarettes with my pianist."

"Cigarettes?" Kiera crossed her arms and kinked her head to the side.

"What? I barely smoke any. Only when I'm nervous."

"Any is still more than none, mister choirboy."

"Choirboy?" If she knew the things I'd done, and the guys I'd done them with... "I think you got your wires crossed there, loopy lady."

"Meh, it was the first singing related word I could come up with." Kiera slid back down to stand on the floor. "Anyway, I think it's crazy you're not making a fortune. You blow me away just singing around the office. I'm thinking I'll forget the hold music and get you serenading the clients. You're amazing."

"Thanks." I kept my focus on my random drawing rather than looking my boss—my bestie—in the eye. "It makes me feel alive like nothing else does. But I'm not getting anywhere. Sometimes, I think maybe it's my sexuality working against me."

"Yeah... because who ever heard of a gay man in the arts? Am I right?" Kiera held her hand up, apparently for a high five.

I shook my head and crossed my arms, another sigh coursing out of me. "I think my real problem is that it's hard to sing love songs with any honesty when I'm chronically single. How long has it been since I had an awesome date? Or even a lousy one?"

Kiera glanced at her hand, still raised as if she was asking a question. Eventually, she spread her fingers and shook them, making a voice-over with a ridiculous French accent. "No, monsieur! You 'ave forsaken meee..." She mimed a time lapse of a dying flower until her hand was flat on the desk.

"You done?" I couldn't stop from smiling at Kiera's antics.

"Yep. Now, we sexy bitches gotta stick together." Suddenly, she stood up straight. "Which brings me back to my point."

"Um, sorry. You're not my type."

"Bitch-boy. My nickname at college was Peggy."

"Um."

"Y'know, because I could strap one on and—"

"Ew."

"Kidding, Gabes. But that's not what I meant, anyway."

"Whew."

"You should come."

"Ew again."

Kiera waved her hands, as if erasing the conversation from an invisible blackboard in front of her. "No, no. I mean, you should come with me on the weekend, to my parents' party. That little shindig is gonna need major distraction. Major." She coughed and turned her focus back to me. "Did I say major distraction? I, uh, meant light entertainment."

"Sounds peachy." I opened my day planner. "Oh, shoot. This weekend? I'm having my toenails ripped out by unicorns."

"Mock me not, olive-skinned demigod. You shall journey with me, and it shall be festive. And you never know what—or who—you might find there." She flashed me a grin.

I quirked my mouth. It wasn't like I'd had any plans outside of a sad movie and maybe a little me-time in the shower, but it still seemed sudden notice to prepare for an out of town gig. "Where are you from, again?"

"A little place called Gray Vale."

"Huh. Never heard of it."

"Nevertheless, you'll love it. It's a step back from the mad pace of the city. Even our airplanes are horse-drawn."

"Are you going to be like this all the time now?"

"Yeah, pretty much."

I tapped my fingers on the desk, searching for any reason not to go. "Will there be bugs?"

"All you can eat."

"Ew. What about wild animals? Lions and tigers and bears?"

Kiera screwed up her nose. "We don't let their sort in. Only wolves... oops."

"Wolves?" I arched my brows.

"Um... forget I said that." She fidgeted with her fingers.

I leaned across and tousled Kiera's russet hair. "Well, you better promise me one thing, curvy red riding hood. Don't let the big bad wolf eat me."

My boss paused, apparently searching for the right answer. "I won't let him do anything you don't want him to." She flashed another cocky smile my way.

"Why would I...? You're just a little weirder than I thought you were, loopy lady."

"Whatevs." Kiera pulled my day planner out of my grip and scrawled all over the Saturday and Sunday pages. "There. It's settled. We leave Friday night."

CHAPTER THREE

Ethan

GRAY VALE HAD barely changed since I'd left. A little bit more crowded, but I put that down to the merger with Stoke Ridge that Kiera had told me about.

The taxi ride from the tiny airport, going through the outskirts and into town, had been more confronting than I'd expected. My few happy memories were strangled by all the others: the teasing and spitting from my peers, and the emotional abandonment by my parents.

As a child, I'd been smaller than most. An easy target, made easier by solitude. My parents were old school, and refused to offer me any protection or respite. Better I died on four feet than lived on two knees. Or some utter horseshit like that.

That had always been the way with the Roddick clan. And almost every other clan in town, if I was honest. It was the law of nature—of wolves—to sort the wheat from the chaff.

I'd retreated into books, and into my own intellect, as much for the refuge they offered as the pleasure they gave me. Bullying was my entire social life, right up until Kiera and her parents learned of my situation and formed a metaphorical wall around me. Protecting me where my immediate family wouldn't.

On one level, I couldn't really fault the system. It wasn't quite kill-or-be-killed, but it was close. And I was living proof that it worked, one way or the other. After all, those who treated me as weak were, in the end, the ones who made me so strong.

I stood in the shadows, at the outskirts of the gathering, casting a wary eye over faces that I'd never expected to see again. Faces that had more often worn monstrous sneers or vicious smiles than anything pleasant.

There was barely a single part of town that didn't hold some bitterness for me. And the less said about the surrounding woods, the better. Time and distance had allowed numbing scars to form on childhood traumas. Even now, as I poked at them, all they evoked were the recollections of pain. Ghosts of hell, and nothing more. But with Clinton, and all that happened...

I growled at myself as the more recent past slammed me in the chest, almost as a physical being. The sense of being truly alone sank deep claws into me, despite my being surrounded by so many others. A lot of the folks were family, though most of them were distant. And that was exactly how I felt.

Distant.

There was a reason I'd stayed away, turned my back on these people. After all, most of them had turned from me first. In the end, though, it had been my choice to leave, and to let this place fade. I'd turned Stoke Ridge into nothing more than a stranger's home movie.

HIS HEALING HEART

When I first left the Ridge I'd thought of my journey as a simple regathering; a way to focus my energies on my career. But time and habit had numbed me to my heritage, to the point I'd let my city life become my only life.

After Clinton, there'd been nothing imaginable to keep me in the place. Not Kiera, not my uncle and aunt, and most especially not my damn parents, who were noticeably—and thankfully—absent from the gathered faces.

Just the thought of them had me reaching for a double scotch from a passing waiter's tray.

"Hi there, tall, dark stranger."

I turned to find my cousin Kiera smirking up at me. I was surprised to feel myself smiling back. Pleasantries over the phone were one thing, but now, face-to-face, everything was that much more real.

And incredibly confronting.

This woman had seen me at my lowest ebbs. Both of them. Though it bonded us deeper than the blood we shared, it was still a barrier. As unfair as it was, Kiera was a physical reminder of just how life could kick me.

I knew it would take my strongest effort not to turn away. To simply head back to the city and wrap myself up in that safe, new life I'd created.

But it was Kiera. Unlike the town, she'd barely changed since I last saw her, and as I released my tension, a tsunami of memories washed through me.

She and her parents had looked out for me constantly. It wasn't as if they'd been much more popular or accepted than I was, with their more liberal views.

Gray Vale style of views, really. They must be loving the new merged pack.

The difference between them and me had been that the Larsons were fucking bulldozers. Nothing stopped them when the whiff of injustice was in the air. And nothing fun had happened in town without Kiera inviting herself, and by extension, me.

Now, years had passed, but the bond was still there, and it was like the bond between twins.

"Hello, Kiera."

"That's it? That's all you got for me after five years? Did your big-city surgeon buddies neuter you or something?"

I held her gaze for a moment before a small bubble of laughter erupted from my mouth. "Well, now I feel at home." I stepped forward and swept my arms around my much shorter cousin, lifting her in a hug that would rival a bear shifter's. "It's wonderful to see you, Killa."

"That's more like it. Now if you could just let me breathe again, that'd be super-great."

I gave her one more squeeze. She was wolf. She could take it. When I placed her back on the ground she gave me a light punch on the shoulder.

"But you're still not forgiven, you big lump. What, did the city lose power or something? All the phone lines were down? Someone broke the interwebs?"

"Yep, that's right. The city elders drafted a plan to get the Pony Express started up again. It probably would have worked, but I ate all the ponies." I took a healthy slug of my unhealthy drink.

"Ugh. Ponies. They taste okay, but they

make me a little hoarse."

My expensive mouthful came straight out into the air, propelled by the laugh I couldn't suppress. "Dammit, Killa. How will I get through this if you won't let me swallow?"

"As the actress said to the shifter."

"Do you have to use that word?"

"What word? Actress? Said? The?"

I simply stared into her eyes.

Kiera stared straight back "You know that steely look doesn't actually work on me, right?"

"I know it never did. I thought perhaps my years of sharpening it might have made a difference."

Kiera hooked her arm through mine. "Cuz, it really is amazing to have you back here. And whether you acknowledge your... s-word status or not, well that's your choice. But hell, it was nice just to hear you joke about your wolf. Makes me think one day you might even embrace him again."

When she looked up at me with such hope in her eyes, it was my greatest temptation to simply lie. Tell her what she wanted to hear.

But in the end, though it would hurt her, I had to tell her the truth.

"I said it back then, and nothing will change my mind, Killa. I am no wolf. Not anymore."

Kiera rested her head on my upper arm and sighed. "All right then, mister serious. Be like that. But it just so happens I brought you a present."

"Me? But it's your mom and dad's special day."

"Well, you know me. I'm a giver."

"If memory serves, that so-called giving was restricted to purple nurples and wedgies, right up until I outgrew your ass."

"If you can't back it up with video evidence, then I'm afraid it never happened. And don't get off the point."

I bopped her forehead with the heel of my hand. "You actually have a point somewhere in all this?"

"Be nice or I'll take my present home with me."

I sighed and took another swig from my drink, making sure to swallow it quickly. "All right then. What could you possibly bring me that I don't already have?"

"Wait here and I'll show you."

"You know I have extremely particular tastes, don't you? In all things."

"Uh-huh. And I know exactly what they are." She shot me a quick wink. "In all things."

Kiera walked off across the clearing, glancing back over at me with that elfin grin that meant she was at her conniving best. In this case, I knew she was drawing out the moment as much as she could, trying to test my patience.

"Test away, Killa," I murmured to myself. "I can stand in one place for ten hours with someone's life in my hands."

I scanned around the gathered clan in a show of nonchalance. There were few other people I'd maybe even consider acknowledging. And only three people who I was certain I'd never met.

As if reading my mind, Kiera stopped right behind one of those strangers, catching my eye and nodding.

I glanced at my cousin, who flashed her eyes wide at me and nodded again at the man she stood behind. Kiera had clearly decided it was time to play matchmaker.

If only she knew what a pointless exercise that was. Hump 'em and dump 'em was absolutely the best I was capable of anymore. Life had given me all the lemons I was prepared to suck.

I raised the glass to my mouth to prevent myself scoffing at Kiera, and her wasted efforts.

The moment I shifted my gaze across, though, I froze in place. The hackles rose on the back of my neck as my blood simmered and surged, pumping through me more like a fist than like a river.

This was not just some random guy. This was a slick, graceful hunk of a man who'd absolutely been designed with the express purpose of tempting me back to the dark side. The side where ridiculous emotional and physical needs ruled. Where libidinous desires stole away a man's ability to think.

On the surface, his tux made him look overdressed, compared to the range of semi-formal attire the rest of us wore. The thing was, he filled it out so damn well, who could argue it was wrong?

The hormonal buzz around him was impossible to ignore, though. Not a woman here who wasn't lusting after the guy, which gave me some pause. I had no idea of his orientation, but the fact that Kiera claimed she brought him here for me had to at least hint he was into men.

As I scanned him from his head to his toes and then back up, my throat constricted. Everything about the man was utterly arresting. The way the light twinkled off his thick, glossy hair. The sweet fullness of his lips and the ready smile that seemed to appear at the slightest provocation. And the kohl of his eyes... dark enough they could match even my soul.

It took only a fraction of a second for waves of want to course through my chest. My lips tingled, sensing the vibrations of the man's own heart as it called across the distance between us.

Even worse, the lust in my belly howled for the succor I'd denied it these past five years.

The hunger of my wolf.

CHAPTER FOUR

Gabriel

AS I LOOKED around, I tried vainly to catch my breath. If I was into women at all, I'd still be a happy camper, but I swore my jaw was about to unhinge in the face of all the ridiculously handsome beefcake in this town. All tall, and broad, and so ruggedly handsome it almost hurt.

I'd long ago come to terms with being

softer and prettier than most men. It sounded like a humblebrag, of course, but that was the way most people saw me.

I got it, too. Like, women across the world would kill for lips like mine. For skin this clear and moves this lithe. I sure leaned into that side of my nature, too, once I realized that owning it was the best defense.

Thing was, it wasn't like I was a small man. In this ridiculous place, though, it was like I was in a trench. Every man I could see, in addition to being hot enough to barbecue my buns on, was at least a half a head taller than me.

I suddenly noticed Kiera standing strangely close behind my back. "Hey, what are you doing back there?"

"My ex is here. I need you to hide me."

"Hide you? With those hips?"

"Oh, you little bitch." She slammed those mighty hips against me, and knocked me sideways. "Anyway, as big you are, you're still the closest to my size. If I hide behind any of these other guys we turn into a cello."

"What are you drinking, loopy lady?"

"Yeah, y'know... he's the fingerboard and the neck, and I'm the rounded body, and together we look... okay, never mind. My uncle's gone, anyway."

"I thought you said it was your ex."

"Why do you think I was hiding?"

"What? Ew."

Kiera shook her head, flashing me that cheeky grin. "Whatever. I was lying, obviously."

"Uh, whatever yourself." I pulled on a lock of Kiera's hair. "Speaking of uncles, you said this is an anniversary party. That means family. You mean to tell me all these human trees here are related to you?"

"For the most part."

I looked Kiera up and down. "So what… it skipped a generation?"

My boss and bestie poked out her tongue. "You be nice, now. Or I just might get one of these trees to fall on you."

"Promises, promises. Do I get to choose which one?"

"Nope. I've already chosen. That's why I was behind you. Marking you for him." Kiera flashed me a lightning fast grin and darted off again, in her usual flighty manner.

I took a quick swig of my champagne as I cast my gaze across the open area. Surely Kiera was joking. Really, what were the chances of finding a hot, handsome guy way out here in the middle of buttfuck? And one who's into guys, as well? Surely that was impossible.

And that was when I saw him.

The man was tall, even by the standard of the gathering. Lush, dark hair, framing a face carved to perfection, but deliciously roughed up by experience. And like me, he seemed frozen in the moment, his square tumbler of whiskey held in suspended animation just below his mouth.

But it was what I saw above the rim of the glass that had me all worked up. His eyes. Silvery gray and fierce as winter, he had those vicious orbs pointed straight at me. For a moment—one that seemed to stretch out through both space and time—the man drilled into my skull from across the clearing.

With three quick swishes, he moved those eyes down and across me, taking in every detail. It was as if he was wielding an invisible knife, slicing the tux straight from my body without even so much as nicking my skin.

I had to curl my fingers into the lapel of my jacket just to be sure I wasn't actually naked. The blatant heat of his gaze left me feeling utterly uncovered. Not just skin deep, either. I swore that man was staring into my bones.

Into my soul.

With that man, I didn't even need my gaydar. I could practically hear his desire as a voice inside my head. As much as I wanted to believe in fate and astrology and all things woo-woo, in my heart I never had. So it was weird to have what felt like a true psychic moment.

I held my breath inside as if it was barbed, and to breathe out would tear me to pieces. Damn. No matter that I hadn't performed yet. No matter that I'd be letting my bestie down. The presence of that big, handsome hunk of pure temptation meant that, as far as I was concerned, this night was over.

Sure, I'd been alone for a while. And yeah, I'd been moaning for a couple of months now to Kiera about there being no good men around.

But that guy?

Hell, no.

That man was not just trouble. He was peril. The kind I really couldn't deal with all the way out here in the sticks.

As if there wasn't danger enough from all the animal predators, now Kiera wanted to dangle me in front of a hungry, hungry hunk as well?

Still the guy stood there, pushing all my buttons from thirty feet away. Buttons I couldn't even reach on my own. Buttons I'd never even thought to look for.

The prickling flames of desire had already started in my cock, and begun to lick their way up my spine and into my head. I could feel the hot, syrupy trickle as my brain liquefied and drizzled all the way down until it took up residence in my balls.

I bit down hard on my tongue, hoping the pain would stem the flow of sinful, dirty thoughts in my fuzzy head. From only three seconds of eye contact, I already knew I was a goner. That I'd climb a tree just to get a taste of that man. Hell, a demigod like that, I'd climb an angry bear to reach him.

And that kind of desperate soul-sucking need simply didn't work with my busy schedule.

Thankfully, a small group of stupidly tall people walked across the clearing between us, breaking whatever spell it was that had me mesmerized. By the time they'd passed, Mister Eyeballs was nowhere to be seen.

For a moment, I entertained the idea that I'd simply imagined him.

A man that perfect?

It had to have been a mirage.

Exactly how many champagnes had I already downed?

As I always did when I drank and got nervous, I pulled out a cigarette from my pocket, noting ruefully that it was my last. As a singer, there was no doubt I should have kicked the habit before ever picking it up, but I was not exactly a man with a whole lot of self-control.

Holding the cigarette tight between my lips, I dug back into my pocket to grab my lighter. And then froze when a deep, smooth voice sounded from beside me.

"Please, allow me, friend."

I didn't even have to look up. Didn't need any confirmation beyond the sound of his voice. It was *him*. The guy who'd sent my thoughts and my morals flying south.

But when I did look up—way, way up—into his eyes, my knees almost failed me, turning to rubber in an instant.

It took more effort than I'd ever known, but I steadied my legs beneath me and leaned gently forward, presenting my cigarette for lighting.

Mister Eyeballs reached out, but instead of lighting it, he plucked the thing from between my lips and crushed it in his huge fist.

"What the hell?" That little cigarette was all that was left of my last gig's pay. And this asshole had destroyed it like it was nothing.

"This is strictly a no smoking affair, man. I'm surprised Kiera didn't tell you."

"But... I mean, you could've just told me. Didn't have to vandalize my property. And how did you know I was here with Kiera?"

"It's hardly an act of genius. She mentioned she had a plus one, and I saw you talking with her."

"Oh."

Every word, every syllable that came from the man's mouth hit like a slap.

Words issued so sharply and coldly they practically left marks on my skin.

If he'd just soften his tone, maybe thaw out that cold, dead heart of his, then that deep, sonorous voice would be like honey-cured sex.

"Look around you, man. It's been a dry year and this town is surrounded by forest. Already there are fires off in the distance. Not to mention there are plenty of sensitive noses here, as you must be aware."

"Well I'm sorry. Kiera never mentioned this was the annual Hayfever Anonymous meeting."

Okay, it had been a smart-ass remark, but you'd think I'd just scratched his Beemer the way he impaled me again with those steel gray eyes. "Are you serious?"

"I tried it once. It never took."

"Kiera didn't tell you about us? This town, these people?"

"Look, Kiera just said she was heading up here for the party, and asked me if I'd come along and sing. It was either this or hosting the Oscars, and who can take that kind of a risk, anymore?"

The big guy narrowed his bladed eyes and sliced through my soul again. "Well in that case, buddy, it would be better for you to simply toddle off to wherever you're staying tonight. This…" He waved his arm languidly around him, indicating the small crowd of nicely dressed people. "This is certainly not a gathering for a sheltered little city boy like yourself."

For a moment, my rage left me unable to form a sentence. All my words tumbled over each other like sweaty wrestlers, each jostling for the right to come streaming out of my mouth first.

"How dare... What the hell do you... I mean..."

"Oh, take a breath, buddy. Then hold it until you've turned around and walked away."

"I will not! Who the hell are you to tell me what to do?"

"Never mind who I am, man. Just trust me on this. It's for your own good." He made a condescending shoo motion with his hand. "Off you go."

Mostly, I was a pretty regular guy. It took a fuck-ton of provocation to get my inner bratty diva rising to the surface. This guy had made it happen in under two minutes.

I stomped my foot and waved my empty champagne flute in the guy's face. "I will not. I'm here for a paid performance. You understand professionalism, mister? Or did you sleep through that lesson in life?"

He simply smirked, his sexy mouth both taunting and tempting me in equal measure. "Trust me. You're far better off being a long way away from us."

CHAPTER FIVE

Ethan

THE BEAST INSIDE me thrashed and howled, threatening to blow my carefully cultivated exterior. In the first days out of Gray Vale and in the big city, my wolf had come close to the surface, drawn out by anything that simply sent my heart racing. It had taken me years of self-control, and as much as possible, controlling my environment, to keep the beast subdued.

Being surrounded almost exclusively by humans had helped, but that didn't explain why everything was turning to shit at that moment. This guy was clearly human, but he had my soul blistering and my mind tingling.

And the creature... the fucking beast was practically bursting through my skin, making demands that were near impossible to suppress.

For me, the matter was beyond question, now. I needed to get this man out of my reach, before I sank my claws—or more likely my teeth—into him. And no way would I condemn this man to that bizarre lifestyle. Even if he knew what being a shifter was all about, and begged to be marked, I couldn't in good conscience do that to him.

He was beyond simply a temptation. His looks, his voice, his dark and sensual eyes, all woke a deep need within me. But it was his scent that had my wolf in a frenzy and scratching at my skin.

Not his cologne or his shampoo. His own natural spicy musk had grabbed a hold of my senses and made my hair stand on end in a way I'd never felt before.

Whoever he was, he held promises I couldn't afford to wish for. I'd sworn off any kind of relationship after Clinton. Even my idle dalliances had been few and far between, and always with men I knew I could never fall for.

While my intellect demanded I cut and run, and fast, my wolf had other ideas. This beautiful man had my senses all riled up in a cloud of red heat. I'd never warred so hard with my beast. My heart circled my mind, searching for a weakness to exploit.

Up close, he was even sexier than from afar. I'd pushed him pretty hard before, just to get him pissed enough to leave. Yet all I'd succeeded in doing was to ignite a robust and fiery anger inside him.

One that made him close to irresistible.

The fire in his eyes spread to the tanned skin of his chiseled face. That sensual peach of a mouth was practically begging for mine. To bite in, to suck the juice from him. To open him up, glide my tongue inside as he pressed his hard, young body against me. I lost myself in the moment, imagining the sweet and languid solidity of his body in my arms as

I drove my cock home, deep inside him.

"Hey, you asshole." The fiery-hearted hottie pulled me back into the moment as he pushed at my shoulders, hard enough to have me stumbling back a step. "Who the hell do you think you are?"

The futility of him trying to use force simply made him even more attractive to me. It showed the fire inside him. A fire I suspected was near unquenchable, and one which my wolf was increasingly desperate to sample.

I quelled the landslide of erotic images coursing through me by downing the last of my scotch. There was no room in my life for the foolishness of a relationship. My efforts to fit in to the human world had been tough enough as a lone wolf. Bringing an actual human into my life was begging for trouble.

But the random, animalistic nonsense roiling within me at that moment was exactly the reason I wanted out of the shifter world. Only then, when I'd conquered my wolf, could I allow myself an indulgence like the one standing before me, eyes ablaze with indignation.

If I could kill the wolf but keep the nose, I'd do it in a heartbeat. If there were a single gland I could remove that would take the beast with it, I'd perform the damn surgery on myself.

But this sexy snack would bring me to my knees. The dark heat in his eyes called straight to my desires. And his scent was off the fucking chain. Part prey, part mate, part meal. Christ, he was just about impossible to resist.

His skin, his hair, and his breath were all rich and delicious. My real problem, though, was the other scent. The one only my wolf could detect.

His cock.

Living in the city, I'd learned early on how to ignore that scent from other people; to turn it into nothing more than a background noise, of sorts. No, this sexy man's scent hit me as a spicy cocktail of sweet and savory, of appetizer and dessert. More than anything, though, his scent was a revelation.

My parents had plenty to answer for in my life. Their passive-aggressive reaction to my sexuality had never surprised me. It was more their flat-out disgust at my choice to move into the human world that hit me harder. Above all that, it was their refusal to allow me a choice of mate, setting me up with one, instead.

And all because of one lie, told to me

before I even reached puberty.

That I had no fated mate.

What better way to press me into the mating they wanted for me, than to convince me I had no other option?

I hadn't even learned this man's name yet, but the way he aroused my human senses—and devastated my wolf's—meant there was no doubt. He was mine.

"Hello?" He poked me again, much more softly. "You in there, butt-face?"

I searched for some way to deal with the moment. Scooping him into my arms and telling him that we were meant to be together forever probably wouldn't cut it. He clearly knew nothing of shifters, or their ways.

"Ethan!"

The familiar voice pulled me out of my internal struggle between wolf and man, lust and reason. I turned to see Abigail Larson beside me, arms outstretched.

"Come on now, handsome. Don't you leave me hanging."

I stepped into the waiting embrace and returned it with genuine warmth. She might be my aunt by marriage and not blood, but Abigail was more of a mother to me than Olga Roddick had ever been.

"It's so good to see you again, Aunt Abigail."

"Oh, hush now, darling. Since when do we have such a formal relationship?"

"Sorry. Abigail."

The older woman moved smoothly out of the hug, but kept her arm looped through mine. She held her hand out to my sexy sparring partner. "Hello, darling. Abigail Larson. And you are?"

"Ethan?"

"Don't be silly, darling. This is Ethan."

The guy shook his head. "Oh, sorry. I'm Gabriel Mendoza. Kiera brought me along to sing tonight." He turned his attention back to me. "You're Kiera's cousin?"

"Yes, but I don't see—"

"See, she told me you were a surgeon in Chicago and I just... uh, pictured you differently."

"You thought he'd be older?" Abigail rested her hand on Gabriel's arm, then drew in a quick breath, turning to Ethan.

"Older?" He coughed and licked his sensual lips, apparently in confusion. "Oh, yes. Older. That's right."

I glanced at the guy—Gabriel—and savored the fresh flush running through his cheeks. I looked at Abigail, whose expression hovered somewhere between surprise and bliss.

With one hand on me and the other on Gabriel, the truth was clear. Her face told me beyond a doubt she detected the same connection I did.

The rapid unfurling of emotion.

The swift heat of blood, pulsing out and in.

The bond between fated mates.

Until that moment, I hadn't trusted my own judgment.

Yet, even though I'd never experienced such an instant and powerful attraction to a man before, I'd been unwilling to truly trust my instincts. That's what I got from trying to deny them, suppress them, for so long.

I trusted Abigail beyond measure, though. If she felt the connection, then it must be real.

Damn it all.

CHAPTER SIX

Gabriel

WHY THE HELL hadn't Kiera warned me that Ethan was pure sex on legs?

Or more importantly, that he was a total jerk?

With all the chatter about him on the drive up to Stoke Ridge, the least my boss could've done was to introduce Ethan to me by name. If for nothing more than to let me know which of the tall, dark, and handsome men I was supposed to be the nicest to.

But instead, all Kiera had talked about was the guy's history. How something vaguely bad happened and he'd turned his back on the place. How this would be his first time back, and she hoped everyone would be nice to him. Or at least civil.

Which was more than he'd done for me. I'd been ready to take a swing at the guy for his rudeness. Hell, I was still bristling with irritation, made worse by that annoying feeling of desperate attraction. But knowing who he was meant I felt I should probably swallow my pride.

With casual violence off the menu, I instead tore a full flute of champagne off the next waiter's tray and took a long slug, letting Abigail keep the conversation going. With any luck, I could just ease quietly into the background and disappear.

Except, as much as I wanted to back away, there was an even greater force at work that kept me close. Not anything I understood, and nothing I'd ever felt before.

Ethan was so fucking gorgeous it physically hurt to look at him without touching. And he smelled just as good. Even though the smoky scent of the distant fires was ever-present, the animal musk of Ethan cut through it all. And hit me like an ocean wave. A body-wide slam of power that was impossible to ignore.

Despite that, I knew turning away was the smart move. Just to keep my distance until I could escape back to the city. That was the safest way to make sure I didn't put my foot in my mouth. Or into Ethan's ass, at speed.

I downed the rest of my drink and got ready to make my quiet exit. I had a gig to perform, after all. Surely, that gave me an excuse to leave.

Abigail interrupted my escape plan, though, hooking her arm through mine and holding me in place. Girl had some real surprising strength in her grip.

Then she rested her other hand on Ethan's shoulder. "A little heads up for you, darling... your parents arrived a few moments ago."

Rather than answer straight away, the big guy raised his glass tumbler and scowled at it when he noticed it was empty. "Thanks for letting me know,

Abigail."

As if the mention of them had been enough to conjure them, suddenly an older couple appeared from the small crowd and walked straight over to Ethan.

"Hello, son."

"Mother." He glanced over at his father's outstretched hand but otherwise didn't move. "Father."

"Come now, Ethan. We've not seen you in five years."

"Well, you know what they say. Time flies when you're shunning sons."

The older man scowled. "Who's been shunning who, boy?"

"Son," his mother interjected. "Please. What happened with Clinton was, of course, rather upsetting. For all of us."

Abigail made a clear move, sliding her hand down Ethan's forearm, which looked to me for all the world like she was marking her territory, which seemed bizarre. After all, these were the man's own parents. "You don't really think any of us can dilute or appropriate this young man's pain like that. Do you, Olga?"

The only answer was a stare with the same intensity as Ethan's. But this one was all ice and no fire.

Ethan's father stepped forward, his arms freshly crossed. "I certainly don't think this is anything for you to concern yourself with, Abigail. It is, after all, a family matter."

"Oh, I see. Now it's a family matter. Whereas five years ago you found his reactions disagreeable and embarrassing. I seem to recall you asserting he should simply grow a pair, as the rather unpleasant saying goes."

"We have certain expectations—"

"No, you have ridiculous prejudices from the Stone Age."

Ethan rested his hand on top of his aunt's and smiled down at her. "Thank you, Abigail. But I can take it from here."

The older woman patted Ethan's cheek, then tugged on my arm, gently drawing us both away from the tense moment. "I think we should get you ready for your performance. What do you say?"

I couldn't help glancing back at the trio as Abigail dragged me away. Okay, so Ethan had been a total asshole to me, but there was no denying how much he messed me up inside.

In the most exciting way.

The fire in his eyes held promise of a heat so powerful it could burn my skin off. Even while he'd been pushing me away with his words, the tone of his voice told a different story.

One of need.

Of desire.

And though I'd wanted more than anything to get myself out of range of his intoxicating scent, and his laser beam eyes, being separated by even a few dozen feet now meant the world suddenly felt cold.

Which was so ridiculous it was embarrassing. To cover myself, I tried to strike up a conversation with my new companion.

"So, Abigail..."

"He's quite a dish, isn't he?"

"What? Who?"

"Oh, come now, darling. Even a jaded city boy would have to be dead not to fall a little bit in love with Ethan."

Christ.

Was I just radiating gay vibes?

Had Kiera told everybody my orientation?

I tried scoffing to deflect how easily Abigail had read my desires. There was no doubt she saw through my charade, and another rush of heat filled my cheeks. "Okay, maybe to look at. But he's such an asshole."

Abigail wavered her head a little. "Oh, I don't know. I do think he was giving you a hard time, but I can't truly blame him for that."

"Well, there's nobody else to blame. You're not going to feed me that tired old boys-will-be-boys crap, are you? That might work for schoolgirls, but it's never worked on men. We were boys, once, remember?"

"Oh, I'm not saying that. He definitely behaved badly, but it was for a very understandable reason. Self-defense."

"What, that big brute was worried I'd scratch his eyes out?"

"Darling, there are far more effective ways to hurt a man than physically. It was just a confronting moment for him. After all, you're everything that boy needs and wants."

"What?"

"And he knows it, too."

"Um, Earth to crazy lady. He was desperately trying to make me leave."

Abigail's laugh was as soft and measured as any other part of her speech. "Oh, darling. Believe me, if you knew his history, you'd know that simply proves my point."

We walked in silence until we reached

the foot-high stage. As I stepped up, I glanced back down at Abigail. "So what, this place is totally full of crazy people?"

Abigail gave me a tiny smile back. "Always room for one more, darling."

CHAPTER SEVEN

Ethan

"ETHAN, AREN'T YOU going to shake your father's hand?"

I glared at my mother in a futile attempt to deter her with my eyes. For a moment, I'd forgotten where I inherited my steely stare from.

"Son?" Hugh Roddick had reached out again. "You're embarrassing me."

I switched my gaze to my father's outstretched hand. "Oh, yes. Embarrassment is a sin that greatly outweighs all others, isn't it?"

"What exactly is that supposed to mean, boy?"

"It means you're both more concerned with how shit looks, than how shit is. Besides, you surrendered the right to tell me what to do when you..." My breath caught in my chest.

"When we what, son?"

I recognized the change in my mother's tone that told me she knew where I was heading. She could always read people far better than her husband.

"When you forced me into that mating."

"Clinton was a fine man, from an ancient clan. You couldn't have done any better for yourself."

"Right. Because who could possibly want me of their own accord?"

"Oh, son, you're mincing my words. I simply—"

"No." I stabbed the air in front of my mother's face. "Nothing you do has ever been done simply, mother. You are the most Machiavellian person I've ever experienced."

Olga glanced across at her husband and then back to me, sighing heavily. "Son, whether you understand or not, the truth is that Clinton was the best mate we could organize for you. The stocks are so much more limited for your kind. Not to mention your... issue, and all."

And there it was. Old time Stoke Ridge shit. I honestly believed they'd have coped with my other problem, if only I hadn't been born gay.

"I didn't need you to find me a mate. Hell, I was only twenty-five. I didn't need a mate at all."

Hugh clucked his tongue. "You were never going to get a quality one. Not while you insisted on slumming with those god awful humans."

"I like humans." I smiled to myself. "But I couldn't eat a whole one." Though with some humans, I'd certainly give it my best shot. I closed my eyes for a moment and pictured that succulent young man whose mouth-watering scent still hung in the air before me.

"Do keep your voice down, son."

I awoke from my reverie and whirled on my mother, speaking through gritted teeth. "Everyone has heard as much of our conversation as they've wanted to, mother. We're all wolves here."

The squeal of a microphone feeding back cut through the clearing, and straight through the consciousness of every wolf in the area.

"Sorry, folks. Technical hitch."

Olga raised one eyebrow as she sneered at Gabriel up on the temporary stage. "Not all of us." She turned back to me with a small shake of her head. "I suppose you'll go chasing after him now, son? You'd do anything just to upset me."

"Mother, there is not a single decision I make, any day of my life, in which your feelings feature at all." I glanced across at my father. "Either of you. You couldn't let me be when I was young. You couldn't support me after Clinton. And you both actively strove to end my medical career before it began."

"Do you blame us? Son, you're putting your hands inside those things."

"Those things? You mean humans, mother?"

"Exactly."

"Oh, you are just too much."

I ran my hand back through my hair as though it could erase the last two minutes of my memory. With a small growl, I turned and marched away.

Olga and Hugh Roddick might be the people who'd spawned me, but they were not my family. And there was no way I'd let them work my anger up to the point where I'd make a scene. After all, though I never formally lived with them, Abigail and Bernard Larson were the ones who'd essentially raised me. And I'd rather miss their party than ruin it.

I'd just reached the road when the

singing started. Up on stage, that delicious feast of a man poured all his worldly desires out into a microphone. Needs, wants, secrets... he'd turned them all into breath, and gushed them through his delectable throat, creating a sensual feast of music.

I froze in place, eyes closed, as the smoky blend of tenor and baritone washed over the clearing, bypassing my ears and spearing straight into my blood.

"No..." My voice was little more than a whisper, and a cracked one at that. As if that slick, handsome man wasn't already temptation enough, he had to go and slice me to pieces with nothing more than his singing voice.

As Gabriel crooned some classic Tony Bennett numbers, I turned back, struggling to keep my hunger under control. It barely mattered that my mind still insisted I get away from him, that I free myself from the spell of that temptation. It seemed my body had overruled me.

Before I knew it, I'd walked to the side of the small stage, taking in every defined but graceful move of his hand as he caressed the vintage style microphone. Fuck, I was staring with the ravenous intent of a pure predator.

I shifted my focus, homing in on his mouth as he formed the words. Lips and tongue working with, and against, each other, like lovers in a perfect ballet.

I closed my eyes and let the man's music pour all over me. The rest of the world faded until all that existed was Gabriel's sexy voice and my fiery blood. And I couldn't tell where one finished and the other began.

All too soon, he sang the last note, thanked the audience and turned off his compact music machine. I took another flute of champagne from the table near the stage and prowled over to where he stood. It was impossible to take my gaze off him as he stepped back down to the ground. He moved like a dancer.

He moved like a wolf. And that should have been enough to make me pause. Instead, I held out the glass toward him.

"Champagne?"

Gabriel turned to me, a supremely bitable smile on his luscious lips. A smile that faded in an instant once he saw my face.

"What, as long as I take it to go?"

I nodded slowly, conceding that one to him. "Oh, come now. Surely we can be civil?"

"I know I can, but then I'm not a jerk." He crossed his arms and shot me right between the eyes with a fierce frown. "Not half an hour ago, you were doing everything you could to get rid of me. I half-expected you to set me on fire, just so you could tell me to go jump in the lake."

I held up a hand, a half surrender. "Please forgive my earlier, caddish, behavior. Is it all right if I call you Gabriel?"

"No. I won't forgive you. What kind of a dumb-ass tries to send someone into exile five seconds after meeting them?"

I nodded, but couldn't keep the smile from curling my lips. It was a struggle to remember the last time anyone but Kiera had spoken to him with such sass.

"I'm afraid that was a

misunderstanding. On my part, by the way, I fully admit that."

"Oh, how big of you. Here, have my room key. Take me, big boy, take me."

The way his scent kept gnawing away at my composure was both heaven and purgatory. My wolf hadn't been so active in years. "I really would like to start fresh. And if I may, to call you by your name."

He frowned at me, but eventually took the offered champagne. "All right. I guess you can call me Gabriel. Anyone who gives me bubbly can't be all bad. And make it up to me how, exactly?"

"Well, I'm afraid I hadn't thought that far ahead. You've kind of made me dizzy with your voice."

The delicious frown on his forehead grew stronger for a moment. "You got some kind of disorder, buddy?"

"Ethan Roddick."

"Haven't heard of that one. Is it like Lou Gehrig's Disease?"

For a moment I paused, before I let a sharp bark of laughter erupt from deep within me. "Oh, you really are a sassy one, aren't you?"

"I have more sass than ass. But that's not so hard, when you have an ass as perky as mine."

I paused for a moment, as my wolf hunched up deep within me, ready to pounce. I'd never had to work so fucking hard to push the beast down. Nor had I felt so close to just giving up that fight. Not since I'd forsaken it, anyway.

In a desperate move to ease my wolf's claim on my mind, I tried a halfway measure. I reached out and stroked my fingers back over his cheek, then rested my hand on the side of his neck.

Though Gabriel watched my hand like it was a loaded gun, he remained still. The only change was in his breathing, which became quick and shallow. It was unlikely he even noticed the change himself, but to my highly attuned senses, it was everything.

"So, Gabriel. Where are you staying?"

"In what world is that any of your damn business?"

"I'm making polite conversation."

"Dude—"

"Ethan."

"Dude, you could punch me in the face and it would still be more polite than your conversation."

"Oh, come now. I'm playing nice."

He took a small step backward, shrugging my hand away. "Exactly.

Playing nice. It's a wonder you don't have pneumonia, the way you keep running hot and cold."

I matched his movements, stepping forward into the small gap he'd made between us. "I've already apologized. I acted terribly, and for reasons I'm unable to explain. But I'd like to make it up to you, if you'll allow me. Perhaps I can show you around town."

"It's dark."

"In the morning."

"I'm sleeping in."

"After you wake up."

"I'm, uh… washing my hair."

"I'll help."

"The hair on my palms."

I burst out with genuine laughter, which felt much more freeing than it should have.

What the fuck had I been doing with my life that a lame-ass joke like that felt like a holiday?

"Well, we'd be a good match, then."

Gabriel stared at me, his face like stone for a few seconds, before he too broke down in laughter. "All right then, butt-face. I suppose I could slum it and allow you to show me around town."

I bowed theatrically. "So, you didn't tell me where you're staying."

"With Kiera."

I nodded, raising my eyebrows. "Really? And how do you know her?"

Gabriel took a sip of champagne before answering. "She's my boss. And my best friend, really. God, that sounds pathetic."

"Hey!" The woman herself appeared, as if we'd conjured her by saying her name too many times. "What's so pathetic about me?"

Gabriel tousled Kiera's hair and smiled. "Not you. Me. That pretty much my only friend in the city is the woman I work for."

"It could be worse," I said.

"Oh. How so?"

I flicked Kiera's ear like I used to in childhood. "You could be related to her."

Kiera poked me in the arm. "Oh, I hope you brought your suture kit, Doc, 'cause my sides just split."

"Do you have insurance? My needle doesn't get out of bed for less than ten grand a day, you know."

"Har-de-har." Kiera leaned in a little closer. "Your mother is asking for you, scrotum-face. My mom and dad are running interference, but you probably should go take care of business."

"I already saw them. I couldn't possibly eat any more shit from them tonight."

"Ethan?" Kiera put her hand on my arm. "Look, I get it. I don't like it any more than you do. But it's been five years, and you really should clear the air with them."

"I'd rather clean the toilet with them."

She was right, of course. I knew my parents well enough to know they expected me to come back home eventually. And they surely assumed I'd take another mate of their choice. At the very least, I had to go and knock that ridiculous notion on the head.

CHAPTER EIGHT

Gabriel

IT WAS STILL nearly impossible to work out if Ethan was some kind of sexy god-like man, or just a complete jerk who happened to be physically perfect in every stupid way. I watched his lithe, muscular body—especially that tight, hard ass of his—as he glided across the clearing toward a small clutch of people.

"You okay, Gabes?" Kiera's warm voice pulled me back into the real world.

"Huh? Oh, yeah. He's just a doodoo-head, is all."

"Oh, that. Yeah. He always has been."

"What's the deal with him and his parents? You all seem such a close family, but it's like he can't stand being anywhere near them."

"We Larsons are close, for sure. Sometimes waaay too close. The Roddicks, though, not so much. It's hard to believe my dad and Ethan's mom were raised in the same house. Uncle Hugh and Aunt Olga are real old-school Stoke Ridge assholes. They're all about social status, and Ethan never matched what they thought their son should be."

"What, because he's gay?" The fire of indignation rose inside me again, only this time it was for Ethan, not because of him.

"No, not that. I mean, they were dicks about it, but they came around eventually. I mean, he's their only cub."

"Ha. That's cute. Cub."

"Uh..." For the first time I could remember, my boss seemed actually flustered. She covered it a second later. "Yeah, anyway, like I say, he wasn't all they wanted, and for stupid reasons."

I tried for a moment to process that concept. "So, wait... he's tall, dark, and ridiculously sexy, in addition to which he's a rich, successful surgeon. Yes?"

"Uh-huh."

"My god, how do they stand the shame?"

Kiera squeezed her mouth into a rosebud shape and crinkled her nose.

"Weird as it sounds, that truly wasn't their plan. When they arranged his mating with Clinton—"

"His what?"

Kiera gulped a quick breath down, and tapped her lips with her finger. "His marriage. What did I say?"

"You said mating."

"Huh. That's weird." She glanced off to the side, at nothing in particular as far as I could tell.

"So, he's married?" Why the hell did that knowledge feel like a cold lump in the middle of my chest? The guy had been ruder than rude to me from the moment I'd met him.

"No, not anymore."

Before I could say another word, a high sound filled the air. Somewhere between a siren and a roar. It wasn't exactly close, but it seemed to come from more than one direction.

"What's that?"

Kiera shrugged lightly. "That's just wolves."

"Wolves?" I tensed up and looked around myself again. "You have wolves here?"

"Like you wouldn't believe, honey."

"You didn't write that in my damn day planner. Head to Stoke Ridge for anniversary. Get throat torn out by overgrown pooches."

Kiera tensed up for a second, then relaxed. "Honey, we haven't had a fatality in years. And that wasn't by a wolf, it was... an accident." She checked her watch. "Well, most of the good stuff has already happened. You wanna blow this popsicle stand? Or would you rather stay around and blow Ethan's popsicle?"

"If you weren't my boss, I'd probably be telling you to go soak your head right about now."

"Is that all?"

"Oh, I guess something about you being a total bitch. Maybe not that wording exactly, but you'd definitely catch my drift."

"Hm. Probably just as well I am your boss then." She struck a cartoonish haughty pose. "Nobody talks to me that way."

"Uh-huh."

"So, which was it? Blow the joint, or blow the man? Want me to flip a coin?"

"How about you flip this?"

Kiera made a show of turning away from my raised finger. "Fine. I can take a hint."

"As long as it's delivered by a marching band, and packed in a luminescent box, with the word *hint* flashing in neon lights on the side of it."

"Yeah, well, whatever works." She turned back as she walked. "Coming?"

CHAPTER NINE

Ethan

WITH EVERY STEP I took, I could sense the tension growing within me, and around me. The gathered throng edged away as I passed by, clearing a path for my hotly radiating anger, until I stood once again before my parents.

Olga was the first to speak. "Hello again, son."

"Don't call me that. Your part-time commitment to me long ago rendered the word inoperable."

Hugh stepped in, his arm raised. "Ethan, some respect please."

"With me, Father, if you have to ask for respect then it's because you've not earned it."

"Come now, boy. It's time you let this Clinton thing go."

I crossed my arms. "Why do you two always assume it's about Clinton? My issue is with you, and predates him by twenty years."

"Oh, dear," Olga hissed. "This is about your darn childhood again. Do you need me to call a therapist, or will a silky-soft hankie do?"

Such cold words from my own mother should have had me firing up. I could feel my wolf within, pawing at my chest as if begging for attention. But knowing Olga's ultimate aim was to draw that very reaction from me helped keep my mind and body steadily human.

"It's a little late for all that, mother. And I'm successful, despite your best efforts. Despite my mate and all that happened."

"Oh, come now. You can't possibly blame us for Clinton."

"Why not?"

Olga took a sip of her white wine and sighed. "Son, you were the only one near him when—"

"I'm not talking about that. I'm saying he would never have been with me at all if not for you two and your damn lies."

Despite my determination, my wolf had his hackles up and was more than ready to pounce. Until this weekend, I hadn't felt so primal in nearly half a decade. But I was not going to let these two drag me back to the life—and lifestyle—I'd sworn off.

"What lies would those be, son?" Hugh crossed his arms and tilted his head in his classic you-have-no-idea stance. "We told the truth about that boy all the way. He was from an excellent family, he was pleasant looking, and he was of mating age. What more could you want?"

"What about love? What about my fated mate?"

Olga waved away my words as if they were meaningless. "Son, not everyone has a fated mate. You were, as you said, already twenty-five—"

"I said *only* twenty-five. Not *already* twenty-five. There's a world of difference in that one word."

"And, quite frankly, it was growing rather tiresome watching you waste your time gallivanting around. Not to mention your distasteful choice in pastimes."

"By pastimes, you mean my surgical career?"

"You know how we feel about that. Surgery is a noble and admirable career."

"As long as I stay away from humans and stick only to shifters."

"That's not true, son," Hugh muttered.

"No?"

"It would be equally distasteful were you to be squelching around the innards of bears and cats, too." He screwed his mouth up. "Oh, don't get me wrong. Bears and cats have their uses, at least. But we wolves are the—"

"Stop it." I was thankful I didn't still

have a glass of scotch in my hand, otherwise I would have crushed it. "I went through with it all, mating with Clinton, because of you two. To appease you. Because you had me convinced he was the best I could do."

"And he was. We're still very good friends with the Milfords. I won't have you speak ill of their son."

"Oh, I'm not. I'm speaking ill of you. What you say is true. Clinton was a fine man, a wonderful wolf. Clever, loyal, and mostly content to be around me." I leaned right in and hissed my anger straight into my mother's face. "But he knew as well as I did, we were not fated for each other."

"Your generation has such a fanciful notion about mating. What I said was true. Not everyone has a fated mate."

"But I do, mother. I just met him

tonight."

For the first time I could recall, my mother's eyes flashed with true anger, and her voice sank into wolf register. "Boy, I know you don't mean that feral little human. I was joking about you chasing him."

"Oh, and you know as well as I do it is him, Mother. Or have your senses deserted you?"

Hugh stepped between the two of us, nudging me backward. "Ethan, you're not thinking straight."

"Ha."

"Sure, humans can be a fun little plaything for a wolf. Not to mention a snack, afterward. But there is no way—"

I held up my hands, halting all conversation for a moment. "Look, I'm not going through this with you two again.

That man is my mate. If you don't like it, then you should make like good little wolves and fucking bite me."

CHAPTER TEN

Gabriel

THE SHORT WALK back to Kiera's family home got my blood pumping again. But more than the exercise, it was the memory of Ethan's eyes and ass that had me short of breath and breaking out in a light sheen of sweat.

As we walked up the hallway toward our rooms, Kiera tapped me on the shoulder.

"Unzip me?" She turned her back, lifting her hair out of the way. As I pulled down on the zipper, I sighed at my own internal conflict.

There was no denying how that man got me all fired up, despite his shitty attitude, but who the hell goes gaga for someone they've only just met?

Kiera turned around and grabbed my bow tie, undoing it for me, and opening my top shirt button as well.

"Oh, mama, that's a relief."

"Penny for your thoughts, honey?"

"The kind of thoughts I'm having will cost you more like $2.99 a minute."

"I knew it, you dirty man-whore."

I poked my tongue out at her. "I thought I told you that was a state secret."

"Not around here, honey."

"What?"

"Well, I don't mean about you being a man-whore. That secret's safe with me and the track team. I just mean about you and Ethan."

"What the hell are you talking about?"

Kiera shrugged as she pushed open the door to her childhood bedroom. "What can I say? People around here are very perceptive. We don't miss much. And it's clear you're super warm for his super form. Taking a class to study his ass. Ready to rock his big ol'—"

"Okay, okay." I shook my head, feeling the frown creasing my brow. "Well, you missed the mark this time. There's nothing between that doofus and me. Got it?"

"Oh, sure. If you say so, Gabes."

I pushed my way into the guest bedroom and stripped off that ridiculous, but still somehow awesome, tuxedo. It was the biggest relief to get out of that thing, despite how sexy I'd felt in it. How sexy Ethan made me feel when he scanned me from head to toe, up and down, over and over, like I was his next meal.

My grey sweatpants and coffee-stained T-shirt might look like they came from a new range of homeless chic, but holy hell they were comfortable. Any time I pulled them on it felt like coming home.

I wandered out to the kitchen where Kiera was making cheese on toast.

"Hey, honey. Want some chow?"

"Nah. Thanks anyway, but I have to hit the hay."

"Lightweight."

I rolled my eyes and grabbed my crotch. "You wouldn't say that if you had to lug around a beast like this."

"Oh, please."

"Hey, you started it."

"No, I mean, please. As in, yes, please, give me a closer look at the goodies, man."

I crossed my arms again and put on my fiercest frown. "The only thing stopping you from being a fellow man-whore is the fact you're not a man."

Kiera mimicked me, crossing her arms and making her big breasts pop halfway out of her loose T. "Who told?"

"Uh..." I nodded at her chest. "The twins kinda give it away, babycakes."

Kiera lowered her gaze to her own chest. "Hear that, girls? This bitch is talking smack about'cha." She cupped her breasts and bounced them in time with her words. "Let's get him!"

"Uh, could your tits shut up for a moment, you think?" I tapped an idle rhythm on the counter. "So, are we likely to have any trouble from those wolves?"

"Which wolves?"

"The ones we heard before."

Kiera smiled and placed her hands on top of mine. "Ah, don't worry about those guys. They were just sounding off. Besides, this house is made from bricks. So, y'know... no amount of huffing and puffing will let them in."

"Ha, ha."

"Although, I'm sure my big, brutish cousin will come save you if you need it. Then we might all hear some huffing and puffing. Eh?" She broke into an evil cackle at her own lame humor.

"You're all class, babe." Before I even

finished speaking, an enormous yawn overtook me.

Kiera reached across and ruffled my hair. "Tell you what, why don't we talk more about it in the morning?"

"Fine by me." I crossed my arms on the surface of the bench and leaned my forehead on them. "Nightie-night."

"Come on, you pain. You can't sleep here. Go to bed."

"Carry me?"

"How 'bout I drag you by the dick, cave woman style?" She snickered for a moment. "Or I could call Ethan and get him to do it."

"Mmm..." Suddenly, I came fully awake and sat bolt upright. "I mean, um... the opposite of mmm."

"Sorry, honey, mmm is a palindrome. I guess you could say it upside down and it'd be www."

"You're not helping, you know?"

"True. But then, I wasn't trying to."

I eased my butt off the bar stool and stretched. "Okay, then. I saw a couple of dust bunnies under my bed. I might get some better conversation from them."

"Good luck. Those two are skanky bitches."

I smiled back over my shoulder as I walked down the hall. "Then they must fit right in."

"Cow."

"Moo."

CHAPTER ELEVEN

Ethan

IT WAS IMPOSSIBLE to tell if I was awake, dreaming, or undergoing some kind of astral traveling. Every inch of my body was drenched in sweat, and something soft filled my fists.

A glance downward showed me I had a vicious hold on my sheets, which helped me rule out the astral traveling option.

Dreaming also seemed unlikely, though my brain certainly wasn't firing on all cylinders. It was almost as if the damn thing had grown a thick covering of hair.

I sat up, rivulets of perspiration coursing down my back and chest. My skin and my core were ablaze as if I'd run a marathon. And I couldn't recall feeling this strong, this vital, since...

Since my first ever shift.

"Damn you," I muttered to my wolf. "You have no place here, anymore."

Clearly, my beast disagreed, the internal snarl growing louder and stronger, and then metamorphosing into a long, fiery howl.

The vibration of the sound, and the spirit of the action, shocked through my body, and I turned my own face to the ceiling, my back arched and my arms spread. It took the act of greatest self-control to keep my voice damped. To hold the roar inside myself.

I should have gone to a motel. Or just headed straight home to Chicago. Instead, I'd stubbornly believed I had my wolf under control. That staying in Kiera's family home—with that hot-blooded, fiery sex-bomb under the same roof—would somehow be manageable. Hell, I'd been so arrogant about my own discipline, I'd even believed it'd be easy.

I might be across the hall and several rooms away from him, but that meant nothing. Not to wolf senses. And his scent was playing hardball.

I rolled out of bed and opened my door. I was so wired that I could almost see the trail of Gabriel's fresh scent. It hooked into me, piercing right through my nose and ears and even straight into my skin. Dragging me toward his room.

It was only the memory of my failings that kept me from descending into the hell of shifting. Even as the beast strove for control, forcing me to fire my hand out toward Gabriel's door, I stubbornly stayed in charge of my feet. I stepped aside, and kept on moving down the hall, away from the temptation.

Every step I took toward the front door had my wolf barking, scratching at me. Its hackles rose beneath my skin, searching for my weakness, desperate to find a way through.

"No," I ground out through clenched teeth. "You are not in charge."

I flung the front door open, letting the cool night air coat me, and suck the furious heat from my body.

Still, that delicious scent reached for me. Long nails of desire scratched down my back, slicing away my resolve. After so long dormant, the creature was full of vigor, but thankfully, unfocused.

I knew I had next to no time. I had to put real distance between myself and my prey.

No, not prey.

Mate.

Clad in only boxers, I leapt from the entrance stairs and sprinted down the driveway, my thoughts focused only on what I was escaping. Nothing about where I was heading.

I kept running through the darkened streets of town, and on out the other side, into the forest. For a few seconds, I paused, caught between anger at the past and fear for the future. In the end, my choices were hacked away from me by pure need, and I charged on into the trees.

As if in defiance of my natural surroundings, every pace took me farther from my wolf, and closer to the man I needed to be.

Still, it appeared my beast had nudged me a little, taking me in good time to Siren Falls.

All I needed was a way to cool the beast inside, and without the slightest pause at the pool's edge, I simply dived straight in and let the icy fingers of the water dig into my flesh.

Below the surface, everything felt beautifully dulled. The pressure of the water both held me in place and insulated me from the world. All I could hear was the white noise of the falls slamming into the pool. It was enough even to subdue my wolf.

I broke the surface and swam for the cascade, soaking up the heavy lances of water that drove into my body as I passed beneath it. I climbed onto the rocks and let the liquid curtain shield me from the rest of the world, while I took the time to control my breath.

And my beast.

CHAPTER TWELVE

Gabriel

DESPITE THE TRAVEL, my performance, and my general fatigue, I couldn't quite tumble over the cliff and into sleep. And I knew it was all the fault of Kiera's big, stupid, sexy lump of a cousin.

Every time I closed my eyes, I saw his. Whenever I touched my face, I remembered how exhilarating—and terrifying—it was when he touched me there.

How was it possible to feel so damn tingly about a guy who could run for President of the United States of Assholia?

When sleep finally did come, my dreams were all messed up, too; full of dark forests and dangerous men. Tall men with tousled hair and broad shoulders. With vise-like hands and shiny white teeth. Ridiculously handsome man-beasts with glowing silver eyes, and who all looked exactly like Ethan.

I came partly awake, my skin wet and my mouth dry. It was like I had a fever, only there were no other symptoms. Just hot blood and hotter dreams that spilled over into consciousness.

Had I gone to bed wearing pajamas?

It was too hard to recall. The only thing certain was that I was naked now.

Within my belly a sparkling pressure rolled and pulsed, as if there was a whole other life inside me.

Was this something like what a woman felt when she was pregnant?

If anything, it felt to me like I had a dormant baby twin I'd shared the womb with, but who'd never fully formed. And now, after twenty-five years, he was suddenly coming to life.

I rolled onto my front and fisted the sheet, burying my face into the pillow. Whatever was happening did kind of hurt... in the same way as a strong fist in my hair during sex would hurt.

Or a perfectly placed swat on my ass.

Soon, the pain grew even sharper, and rose from my core to the center of my chest. I rolled out of bed and onto the floor, landing on hands and knees and letting my head hang low. The closest thing I could compare this sensation to was muscle cramps, only this time it covered every single inch of my body. Even my hair and nails screamed with the pain.

And yet, it wasn't actually an unbearable sensation. Just unexpected and huge. Like getting into a hot bath too quickly.

Or taking a sweet, thick cock you hadn't quite warmed up enough for.

I raised my head and glanced around myself. The near dawn light filtered in around the drapes and gave my eyes enough to work with.

My rapid breath fired in and out, and I gritted my teeth around it, sensing the need to get my damn self under control.

A moment later, I heard a series of light thuds in the hallway, and my heart punched me in perfect time with the rhythm. I scrambled to my feet and opened my door, staying as silent as humanly possible.

It wasn't clear in my mind what I'd expected to see. But one thing I'd never anticipated was Ethan, nearly naked and soaking wet, prowling up the hall away from me.

I'd meant to stay silent, but seeing his hard, muscular body, wearing nothing but boxer shorts made translucent by water, hauled a sinful, needful, desperate moan straight from my throat.

The big, beastly man halted instantly, and I froze, unsure if it was fear, desire, or some otherworldly force that held me immobile.

Ethan turned on the spot and fired that glowing silver gaze of his like a crossbow, impaling my heart and my senses instantly.

Only then did I remember I was completely naked.

To my shock—and delight—Ethan curled his lip and made a deep, gravelly sound as he took a step toward me. I could have sworn it was a growl.

An honest-to-goodness animal sound.

As he prowled my way, the fluid sway of his mighty shoulders made me dizzy, and as he picked up his pace, I widened my eyes in genuine fear.

A moment before he would have reached me—maybe even attacked me—I slammed the door and locked it, diving onto my bed and pulling the covers over my head. The way I used to do when I was six, and hiding from the big, bad wolf.

And other monsters.

To my surprise, there was no heavy slam against my door. No angry pounding of fists, or yelling of demands. It was as if the man had never been there at all.

And as I fought to bring my heart and breathing back under control, I was left wondering if I'd simply dreamed it all and had only just now woken.

CHAPTER THIRTEEN

Gabriel

WHEN I NEXT opened my eyes, bright sunlight had created a warm glow in the room, creeping in around the outsides of the drapes.

I slipped out of bed and crept to the door, putting my ear against it as if the big, sexy beast who'd scared the life out of me last night might still be there. Resting on the other side, listening for me. His hot breath rasping in and out, as he desperately clawed at the thick wood.

If he'd actually been real.

But of course, I heard nothing of the sort. Just the general clink and clatter of people fiddling around in the kitchen.

I threw on my light cotton robe and nervously headed out, still trying to unravel the maze of experiences from the night before. And still unable to decide how much of it—if any—was real.

Kiera sat at the breakfast table, but to my dismay, she wasn't alone. And of course, it had to be *him* sitting beside her. The two of them were obviously talking to each other, but so low that I couldn't hear them, even from only a dozen feet away.

Thankfully, it was Kiera who spotted me first.

"Hey, Gabes. Sleep well?"

My boss had a slightly crooked grin, and not for the first time, I grew suspicious of the woman. She might be my bestie, but Kiera never missed an opportunity to poke fun. And here in Stoke Ridge, the girl constantly looked as if she was the keeper of a hundred different secrets.

Combining that with the fact she'd just been whispering to that man, and I was ready to scuttle back into the guest room and stay there until I could ease the heatwave inside me. Which, if Ethan stayed around, could take weeks.

Months.

"Gabes?" Kiera's repeated question finally cut through my thick jungle of confusion.

"Um, yeah. I think so. I had a... a

weird dream." It had to be a dream. Because if it was real, I didn't know how to process all the feels I'd be having.

I took a seat at the counter and leaned my face on my forearms. "Any plans for the day?"

"I don't, but you do."

"I do?"

"Uh-huh." Kiera flicked Ethan's ear, the way he'd done to her the night before. "This lump said he promised you a tour of the town."

The big man smiled and focused those twin silver weapons on me. "So that'll be the first hour taken care of."

Kiera bumped him with her shoulder. "Be nice. Stoke Ridge has plenty to see and do. Especially now we're a part of Gray Vale and all. Why, you could make that tour last as long as ninety minutes."

I desperately needed to change the subject, and especially the itinerary. Being alone with that man, even for an hour, would be the most heavenly torture. Despite the rocky start to our meeting, Ethan was growing more and more impossible to resist.

The worst part was, my desires were interfering with my natural thoughts. It was hard to be snarky and rude when your damn mind was in your balls all day long.

Whether the night before had been a dream, a reality, or something in between, shouldn't matter at all. I definitely could not let the man get to me.

"Is that coffee I smell?"

"Allow me." Ethan stood, the simple movement seeming to fill the room. "How do you take it?"

"Orally."

Ethan paused for a few seconds, before continuing over to the coffee maker. "Good choice. Shall I give you a shot of cream?"

"Dammit. I should've seen that one coming."

Ethan had his mouth halfway around a smart-ass reply when Kiera interrupted. "Quit it, you two, or I'll hurl right now." She looked over at Ethan. "He takes it with one long squirt, and two sweet lumps."

I struggled to suppress my laughter. "Speaking of hurling."

Ethan prepared my coffee and placed it in front of me.

"Thanks, butt-face."

"You know, you can call me Ethan, if you want."

"Noted."

I wasn't striving to be rude, but I also didn't want to let my ridiculous desires show. More than anything, I desperately wanted to ask about the night before. Whether I'd been dreaming, or if Ethan had actually been prowling around, soaked to the skin, in just a pair of boxers.

Boxers that clung to his ass like a jealous lover.

The way I'd do, if I ever got the chance.

Oh, god.

I definitely needed to push those thoughts way, way down into the background. The memory of that liquid sheen on his skin, and the smooth rubble of his abs. The hard V that ran inward and down from his hips. All of it mixed in my mind and the cocktail of lust had my balls simmering. And my cock pulsing with want.

At the same instant, Ethan and Kiera both hummed, as if they'd simultaneously come up with a good idea.

"What's going on, you guys?"

Kiera was the first to move. "I, uh... have to take some, um... things to, uh..."

"To that place," Ethan finished. "That place with the stuff."

"That's the place," Kiera said as she scurried out of the kitchen. "The place with the stuff. That's where I have to take my things."

And just like that, I was marooned. Trapped in the kitchen with the sexiest man I'd ever seen, heard, or touched.

Or dreamed, for that matter.

CHAPTER FOURTEEN

Ethan

THE THUD OF Gabriel's heart was part heaven and part hell. It pounded into my ears like a drum, and fired straight into my brain. The fact I could hear it straight from the source, and also sense the way it had his cock dancing, only made it harder to ignore.

The trouble was, it bypassed my

human side and latched onto my wolf, tugging him by the tail, by the teeth, and by the nose. Jealously and relentlessly dragging that beast toward the surface.

Clearly, I hadn't imagined it, either. The moment I'd detected Gabriel's cock hardening, Kiera had obviously noticed it as well. Thankfully, my cousin had removed herself from the situation in a heartbeat.

"So," I continued, struggling to form thoughts, let alone actual words. "I'm still available for that tour, if you want. Don't feel pressured or anything."

Gabriel licked his sensual lips, holding my attention with nothing more than that tiny gesture. "I suppose it might be nice."

Even in plain speech, his voice held me rigid. Though it just might have been the slight wavering in his tone, as much as the honey-smoked warmth, that had me ensnared in his being. The sexy spark in his eyes, the sass in his words, the hard planes of his sexy body showing clearly through that thin robe... every moment I spent near him, ground away at my resolve. If I simply released my darker self, abandoned my years of discipline, then all I could envision was a complete mess.

Emotional chaos, lustful indulgence, sensual overload.

So why did that particular kind of mess have my mouth watering and my breath shallowing... and my wolf snarling like hell?

It had taken all my will, plus a long run and a cold swim, to force the animal down last night. And even after all that, it took no more than a fleeting glimpse of him, a soupçon of his scent, to get the beast pushing through my skin again. Sinking its teeth into my mind.

The smart thing truly would be to turn tail—metaphorically speaking—and flee back to Chicago. Disappear and keep him thinking I'm an asshole, rather than sticking around and leaving him in no doubt.

I'd finally managed to convince myself to do exactly that—leave town in a hurry—when he raised his arms and stretched out the kinks of sleep. Baring his most vulnerable pulse points to me, as if daring me—begging me—to sink my teeth into him.

The hackles rose on the back of my neck as I studied his hard-bodied magnificence through his robe. The tender, stubbled skin of his throat, his blood visibly pumping within, called to me like a feast.

I knew instantly I was utterly lost in him. That even though I could never allow myself to take him as my mate, he was burned into my brain forever.

With that knowledge came a surprising sense of freedom. I had planned to scamper home to escape the pull of Gabriel's pure essence. But, since he'd immediately and permanently spoiled me for all other men, then things really couldn't get any worse.

What would be the harm in staying a day or two longer?

"All right, Gabriel. How about I start the tour with breakfast in town?"

As soon as I mentioned food, his belly set about growling in earnest. Somehow, it even sounded as if it was singing a harmony to the wolf in my heart.

"Um... that might be nice."

CHAPTER FIFTEEN

Ethan

IF I'D HAD any doubt over how perfect Gabriel was, watching the way he savored every bite of his food would have blown those doubts out of the water. Bacon, sausage, eggs, tomato. Toast with butter, coffee with cream. And with that voice straight from heaven, every noise of appreciation he made seized me simultaneously by the heart, and by the cock.

He seemed to realize suddenly that he was the main attraction. At least, to me he was.

"Am I amusing you, butt-face?"

"Ethan."

"I know. Is this some kind of cabaret for you, big guy?"

I used a sip of coffee to suppress my grin.

Hot-blooded little fireball, this one.

When I spoke, I kept my voice low—in pitch as well as volume.

"There's simply nothing quite like a man who appreciates his food." I paused for a moment as I weighed up my two sides—wolf and man—and tried to understand which part held the most sway. And it was impossible for me to know at that moment.

"I have a singer's ego to feed. So sue me."

Barely even thinking of what it meant, I slid my hand down on top of his. Only when the electrifying jolt ran from his body and into mine was I reminded just who we were to each other.

"I know you're making a joke at your own expense. And maybe it's to deflect some of the doubts you won't admit you have." I leaned closer, dropping my voice to a raspy whisper. "But I see you, Gabriel. More than you'd like to admit."

The rich tan color of his face reddened as the heat of my words registered. He pulled his hand free of mine and glanced down at the plate. When he looked up again, the fire in his eyes nearly cooked me on the spot. I still couldn't be sure if it was anger, arousal, or the perfect blend of both.

"Was that real last night?"

"Which part?" I asked, feeling certain I knew what he was talking about.

"In the hallway. You, prowling around in your undies like a perv."

"What do you mean, *like* a perv?" I gave him a tiny wink, and my heart leapt when the corner of his mouth curled up.

He stabbed his fork into a sausage and pointed it at me. "You still didn't answer me, butt-face."

I nodded, and placed my coffee on the table. "Honestly, I wasn't entirely sure myself. For all I knew, I'd dreamed the whole thing, but the fact you asked me that tells me it must have been real."

"So what were you doing?"

"How much do you know about Stoke

Ridge, Gabriel?"

He narrowed his eyes and pointedly bit through the sausage on his fork. "Don't change the subject."

"I'm not. Not exactly. But if you don't know the secrets of this place—of the people here—then it's almost impossible to explain."

Gabriel frowned, a perfect, kissable kink forming between his eyebrows. "Is this a cult, or something?"

"It's an or something." I put two twenties on the table and stood. "You ready for the tour?"

Gabriel gulped the last of his coffee and stood. "Fine. But we're not finished discussing this, pervy-man."

"Well, we'll see. Things might become clearer as we explore the town."

CHAPTER SIXTEEN

Gabriel

WALKING WASN'T REALLY one of my chosen activities. There was so little need for it in the city, with taxis, ride shares and—ew—buses. Hell, sometimes I was surprised I even had a pair of sneakers.

And yet, the hot spots and aches that had sprung up across both my feet somehow weren't enough to make me call time on this little diversion. As long as I had Ethan's delicious body beside me, and the heat of his voice filling my ears, I felt as if I could keep ambling along all day and night.

What the hell was up with that?

And why was it that every time that gorgeous man made the slightest contact with my skin, it felt as if my legs had turned to liquid?

The tour itself had been pretty uneventful, just as he'd promised. Or maybe *warned* was a more appropriate word. We'd barely run across anyone else, and Ethan had been coldly dismissive of those we had met. I desperately wanted to ask him what his problem was, but after the party last night, I couldn't be sure it was truly *his* problem.

I'd only briefly encountered the man's

parents, but already I didn't like them. I got a real strong feeling they were pretty cold about me, as well. Every other person I'd met, apart from Kiera's family, had seemed somehow cut from the same cloth. As if they felt Ethan had to somehow prove his worth to them.

"So, that's that." His deep voice cut through my thoughts. "Unless you feel like heading down to the old Gray Vale area."

I glanced around myself. We'd apparently gone through every part of this small town. I looked across at the thick forest on the other side of the street.

"What about in there?"

"It's not safe in there. Not for a city boy."

"Oh, please. You haven't seen the back alleys around my apartment building."

I started crossing the street, but before I'd taken more than a few steps, Ethan grasped my shoulders in his big, strong hands.

"No, Gabriel. I mean it. There are dangers in there that I… I can't describe to you."

"How dangerous can it be when there's a damn candy store across the road from it?"

He frowned as he clearly tried to sort through his thoughts. Eventually, he sighed and released me. "People here are… well, we're used to the dangers these woods present. It's like, if you grow up here, you're kind of inoculated."

"Doesn't look any different to any other forest I've seen."

"That's the danger."

I crossed the street, stopping at the

edge of the woods. I reached out and combed my fingers through the leaves on the closest branch. A cool breeze ran through the treetops, sounding for all the world like a whispering voice.

I sensed Ethan's bulk behind me, and I closed my eyes to block out sight, and call on all my other senses. Rather than danger, I sensed a warmth before me. Somewhere between a log fire and a thick quilt.

At that moment, a group of children came running out of the underbrush, dressed in nothing but swimsuits. They paid no attention to either of us, simply scampering up the streets and into various homes.

I glanced back at Ethan.

"Dangerous, huh? So dangerous that little kids run around in there. Without any kind of protective wear."

"Just proves what I said. You grow up here, you understand it."

"Will you take me in there? A big, bad man like you would surely be able to protect a soft city boy?"

Immediately, Ethan's face closed down. As if he'd built a brick wall in front of it and pasted on a picture of his frowniest face.

"No, Gabriel. I won't." He took my hand and gently steered me back toward the center of town. "I'm not making this up. There are things in there you can't understand."

I reached up and knocked lightly on the side of his head. "There's plenty in there I don't understand either, big man."

"That's probably for the best."

Though he'd clearly meant it as a joke,

there was a coldness in his voice that had my entire body tensing up again.

I cast one more glance back at the forest before Ethan steered me around a corner and I lost sight of it.

***

Sleep proved just as elusive as it had the night before. And for the same reasons.

Every time I closed my eyes, those two silver bullets of Ethan's pierced my mind. My whole body thrummed with an electricity that apparently couldn't be switched off.

The sheen of perspiration was back, too, along with the volcanic heat inside me. Every inch of my skin was awash, and my cock stood tall like a fucking main mast on a ship.

What the hell was happening?

Was it something in the water?

In the woods?

Or was it that damn man and his ridiculously sexy everything?

I kicked away my sheets and blankets, seeking relief. This time around, the sensations were much more like genuine pain, as if the previous night had been nothing more than an undress rehearsal. Or maybe my soul was bruised all over from the pummeling this experience had given me. It felt as if the slightest touch would ignite every part of me—mind, body, and soul.

I curled into a ball and then rolled over onto my belly. Still the pain gripped me like a gigantic fist. I squeezed my thighs together and pulled my knees forward, propping my ass high, arching my back downward in a deep stretch. The cool night air kissed my puckered ass hole like a lover, and somehow, the combination of cool air and stretching eased the hurt.

The sound of my bedroom door opening sang to me like music, and the musky scent that filled my nose was heaven. Two parts nature, three parts man. Water and forest and the spicy tang of maleness. A low growl escaped his body and it coated my back like it was licking me.

The weight of him as he mounted the bed behind me sent my balance swaying. He curled his hand out to my hip and rested it there, velvet soft and blazing hot. It was a nothing touch, a place he'd easily put his hand if we were clothed and dancing. Yet it drove deep, long roots of want through my entire body.

When he put his other hand up

around my shoulder, I lost any pretense of being a big, strong man. I basically mewed like a kitten. He tightened his grip, as if he thought I might flee.

Truth be told, I'd already thought of doing so a thousand times. But running only gets a guy chased, and there was no chance in hell I could ever outrun this man. Not with those long, hard legs, and that cold fire burning inside him. Nor could I escape my own white-hot desire to have him.

Right then and there.

If this was even real.

My mind was a ball of fuzz, and it was just as impossible this time around to tell if I was living a dream. My mind had always had the knack of revealing my wildest desires when I slept.

Ethan—if it truly was Ethan—slicked

his hand down from my shoulder and through the indent of my spine. He brought a pool of sweat down and it washed over my willing little pucker.

When he jammed his thumb against me, I gasped, amazed at how soft and open I already was. Like my body had been waiting for him since the moment I'd arrived in Stoke Ridge.

He glided his thumb inside me, and I moaned with the sweet pleasure, tempered with only a minor sting of pain. I even bounced back at him, trying to take him deeper. Readying myself for the beast I knew he was packing.

If it really was Ethan.

A moment passed, and then he slipped his thumb out and gripped my shoulder again as he notched the blunt head of his cock against me. I took a long breath in, holding it. When he drove forward, filling me so fucking easily with his heat and terrifying me with his howl, I let the breath slice its way out of me.

As big as I was, this man effortlessly bumped me around like I was no more than a puppy. He glided that perfect, thick cock of his in and out, squeezing my flesh with those powerful hands. His deep voice rolled out in bitten off growls, like it had taken a physical form and begun chasing me through a thick forest, stepping around every obstacle between us, until it could bury its fangs into me.

His weight pushing down on my back, thumping into my ass, was fiercely erotic. I tightened around him with a whimper and his voice evaporated into nothing more than a steamy hiss. The sheen of sweat over my body made his hand slip, and he released my shoulder, taking a fistful of my short, thick hair instead.

As he slammed himself home inside me, he dragged on my head, pulling hard, blessing me with the sweetest pain across my scalp. I lifted my body from the bed, and he drew me up and back until my shoulders slammed into his chest. I still hadn't so much as looked at him, but when he took my neck between his teeth and squeezed, I couldn't even think about opening my eyes.

He slid his hand around my hip and gripped my steely cock, all the while licking and sucking at the flesh of my throat. If it was still a dream, then I needed more than anything not to wake up.

Like, ever.

Every pump of his hand up and down

my raging boner simply detonated within me, driving pleasure up my spine and turning into fireworks inside my head. The wet glide of his cock filling me fired bullets of ecstasy into my blood, and in seconds my entire body tingled in anticipation.

And when his voice returned, a deep, rasping growl, it filled my head, wiping out thoughts of everything but this man... this beast.

With one final punching drive, he slammed home inside me, so hard he lifted my knees from the bed and balanced me on top of his hips. His grip on my hair tightened, sending blissful spikes of sensation down to meet the flames of orgasm erupting from below. The two forces came together in my chest and I swore I was about to burst.

The heat of his fluid cascaded deep inside me, just as he hauled my own release from within me. I fired off like a cannon, painting my sheets and pillow with my juice as I had the biggest climax I'd ever experienced.

As his climax gradually eased, he let me slide back down to the bed. I was nothing more than a lump of pastry, rounded and pounded, kneaded and folded. And I'd need to rest a looong time before I'd be ready to rise.

Without a word, he slid down behind me, his skin still deliciously, blisteringly hot. The last thing I remembered before unconsciousness overtook me was his big, strong arm curling around my body.

CHAPTER SEVENTEEN

Gabriel

I WOKE WITH a start, looking around the room. Though I was alone, it was hard to figure out if that was surprising or not. Sunlight streamed through the cracks in the blinds, landing on the smooth, carefully made blankets covering me. The blankets I swore I'd practically torn to shreds the night before in my desperation to ease the fever inside me.

I ran my hand across my face and scrubbed, trying to sort dreams from memories, reality from fantasy.

Was that mystery man real, or a figment of my horny imagination?

And more importantly, was it Ethan?

I'd felt that weird feverish heat all through my body before he came to me, just as I had the night before. But maybe even that had been just part of a dream.

There was only one thing I was certain of; if I'd only imagined that wild sex, then that would turn out to be the biggest disappointment of my life. But I was alone now, and there was not a single sign around me that anything had happened. Even the bed covers were still mostly in place.

It was only as I tried to get up that my

questions found some kind of answer. My arms and legs ached, which surely was a sign I'd been fucked relentlessly. Although, I guess it could easily be from the walking tour.

I finally managed to lift my weary body from the sheets, and sure enough, I found the remnants of my release, smeared into the sheets by my body as I slept.

But still nothing that made it clear anyone else had been with me. Fuck, maybe they just pumped hallucinogens into the guest rooms here, for fun. Just to see how city folk freak out when they come out to the sticks.

The delicious, keening pang in my ass, though, had to be proof enough that everything I'd felt last night had been real.

But with that knowledge came the memory that I'd never even looked at him.

Never challenged him. Just let him prowl into my room and take me from behind. I'd been a man-whore before, but at least I made the guys work for it back in the city. Last night, I'd given it up like I owed it to him.

And it had been so fucking perfect it hurt.

From the moment I'd felt the heat, from the moment that man had busted into my room, I'd assumed it was Ethan. But after all, this was Kiera's family home.

What if it had been Mr Larson?

Celebrating his anniversary by switching teams and banging his daughter's plus one?

"Oh, god..."

As embarrassing as that might be, would it really be any better if that was

Ethan's incredible body grinding into mine?

He was arrogant, aloof, and clearly had a roll of razor wire strung around his mind and his heart. Not to mention he was cockier than a rooster farm, and lived in a whole other city, in a whole other state. Nothing could ever happen between us.

I slowly rolled out of bed, dragging a robe on and stumbling to the kitchen. Kiera was already up and far chirpier than anyone had the right to be so early in the afternoon.

"Here you go, honey." Kiera handed over a fresh-brewed coffee. "Wanna talk about it?"

"About what?"

"Last night, of course. You and Ethan. I think we're gonna have to replace a couple windows."

"W–what are you talking about?" So, it had really been Ethan. Trouble was, that meant it had really been Ethan.

Leaning across the counter, Kiera cupped my face in her hands. "Honey, honey, honey. You're in wolf country. Ears don't lie, especially..." She paused for a moment, as if weighing up whether to continue. "Especially ears like ours. But seriously, regular folk two counties away would have heard you guys."

"Oh, god." I pulled out of Kiera's grip and covered my eyes. "It was bizarre. I couldn't even tell if it really happened or not. It felt like a dream all the way through."

"That's normal, Gabes."

"Not for me. When did I become such a trollop?"

"Trollop, schmollop."

"I mean, I just don't do that."

"You don't do it? Why ever not?"

"Sex? Sure. I do it every chance I get. It's just that lately, every chance has pretty much been zero." I took another fortifying gulp of coffee. "But this wasn't even like sex on the first date. I mean, sure, he showed me around town, but then we came back here and I didn't see him again. I think he went back out."

"Still kind of like a date. If that makes you feel better?"

"No. I mean, I was trying to sleep, but it was too hot. He busted into my room. There was no talking. No foreplay. Just…"

"Just glorious, mind-scorching, sheet-ripping jiggy-jiggy?"

"Exactly. It's embarrassing."

"Why? I told you, wolf country. Sex is

as natural as eating around here. And sometimes, it's hard to tell where one ends and the other begins."

"What the hell are you talking about, Kiera? You keep bringing up wolves and talking like... I don't know. Like you're completely deranged."

Kiera frowned as she poured herself a cup of coffee. "I know. I've been dancing around it, but I guess it's time to 'fess up. It's clear Ethan hasn't told you yet."

"Told me what?"

Kiera placed her cup on the counter and leaned forward on her crossed forearms. "This entire town, including me and even my knucklehead cousin... we're all wolf shifters."

"You're what?"

"Wolf shifters. You've heard of us, right?"

I sipped at the blissfully hot liquid in my cup. "Is that like a moving company? The Wolf family and their fleet of lorries?"

"No, honey. Humans who become wolves."

For a moment, I screwed my mouth up to the side. "You mean role playing? I had an uncle who, like, dressed up in costume to go watch Harry Potter."

"And what a fabulous uncle he must have been. But no, not role-playing. I mean we literally turn into wolves."

I glanced around. "Okay, where's the camera?"

"There isn't one."

"We've been having a busy time at work. Maybe your brain snapped?"

Kiera chuckled and wrapped her hands around her cup, leaning forward on the bench. "Nope. I'm as sane as you are."

"Not sure that's exactly a glowing endorsement, you know?" I took a longer slug of the coffee and gave Kiera a double shot of side-eye. "So, what... you're trying to tell me shapeshifters are real?" I couldn't keep the grin off my face.

"Absolutely. It's not exactly a huge secret. But on the other hand, we don't go around blabbing it to everyone we meet, either."

"So, you just, kinda, turn into wolves and go off to play with Bigfoot?" I chuckled at my own joke. "Oh, do you have, like, changing rooms? So you can get into your wolf suit in private?"

Kiera rolled her eyes and smiled. "Now you're being silly."

"Oh, yeah. I'm the one being silly. When you're the one claiming to be a vixen."

Kiera sucked in a quick breath and flared her eyes. "Vixens are female foxes."

"Yeah, yeah."

"No." Kiera stood right in front of me, hands on hips. "Not yeah, yeah. I'm a wolf, not a fox. What you just did... well, it's like telling a Trekkie to use the force."

"Calm your tits, babe. What's wrong with foxes?"

Kiera sighed out so hard it sounded like she was deflating. "Nothing. It's just that I'm not one."

"I know." I put my hands around my mouth in a mock yell. "Because you're a human."

Kiera remained still for a moment, one eyebrow cocked. "All right. I guess there's only one thing for it." She pulled her T-shirt off and started unbuttoning her jeans.

"Hey, look, I love you, Kiera, but only as a friend. You understand?"

"Pfft. I'm not getting naked, I'm just taking off all my clothes."

"Because there's a difference, of course. But the real question is, why?"

Kiera was down to just underwear by that stage. "You ever tried to unclip a bra without your hands?"

"You, uh… remember who you're talking to, right?" I fist-pumped the air. "Gold star gay boy here."

With Kiera now stark naked in front of me, I wasn't sure where to look. Okay, so the girl was curvy and gorgeous, but even in college I'd never tried swinging with the straights.

"Are you ready, Gabes?"

"Ready? For what?" If she said sex…

"Watch."

I kept my gaze locked on Kiera's, mainly because that was a little bit less uncomfortable than looking any lower. The comfort was short-lived, though. After a moment, something freaky started going on with the girl's body.

"Told you... it was truuue..."

As I watched, Kiera's face bent out of shape, elongating in front as her ears migrated up her head. She dropped to her hands and knees and grunted, as weird popping noises and horrible cracking sounds erupted from all over her body. Before I could truly comprehend what was happening, there was a gray and ginger wolf standing in the kitchen of Kiera's family home.

For a moment, I sat still, gaping at what had happened. Then wolf-Kiera nuzzled at my hand, like a pet dog might, and the spell was broken.

"You gotta be fucking kidding me. How did I not know this about you? About anyone?"

The sound of a door opening down the hallway set wolf-Kiera into alert mode. She raised her ears and turned, stalking toward where the sound came from. Kiera's mom called out, sounding even more tired than I had earlier.

"Morning, you two."

A moment later the sound of the shower running seemed to put wolf-Kiera at ease. With her tail still pointing at me, and with the same disgusting noises, she morphed back into human form, finishing up on all fours.

"Um..." I studied my fingernails. "Uh, Kiera?"

"Wh–what?" She panted heavily, like she'd been running.

"Well, I know you're a wolf and all, and you guys are really keen on the moon... but, uh..."

Kiera glanced over her shoulder with a smile, then wiggled her ass. "Aw, mister Gabes is all confronted."

"Hell yes, I am. My best friend just flashed me everything she has. Oh, and did I mention she turned into a goddamn wolf?"

Kiera stood up and shrugged her clothes back on. "Yeah. I should have told you before we made the trip. My bad."

"Yeah, you should've. Wait... you said Ethan is a wolf, too?"

Kiera paused for thought. "He's more of a lapsed wolf, really. It's not something he talks about. Not even with us."

"Yeah, I noticed he has a select few topics to talk about. And a bunch of no-go zones." Of course, after his performance in my bed last night—all action, no words—I could argue that talk was hella overrated.

The fact I was ranking mindless sex above a meaningful relationship had me feeling like I needed to add yet another point to my whore score.

"All right, so what the hell is with him, anyway?"

"It's a long story. I can tell you some, but not everything."

"Spill! If he can do that, what you just did, why the hell doesn't he do it all the time? Why don't all of you?"

Kiera screwed up her mouth as she shrugged. "What, aside from the effort it takes? Well, there are times it's just better to be in human form. Job interviews, meeting people's parents, BDSM clubs. You know."

"What the hell?"

"It is so damn hard to get a good swing with a riding crop when you have to hold it in your mouth." She caught my expression and held up her hands. "I'm kidding. Sorry."

"You better be."

Kiera shook her head with a smile and continued. "But Ethan? Man, you could barely stop him shifting when he was a kid."

"I don't believe that."

"It's true. He was a wolf more often than—"

"No, I don't believe that guy was ever a kid."

Kiera smiled and stood up. "Come on,

this kind of story needs to be served with a side of food and booze. Go get dressed."

"Don't wanna."

"Well, if I'm gonna spill about your bed-buddy, then I want to do it somewhere he isn't."

I felt my guts ice up. "Oh, god. I forgot he was staying here."

"Uh-huh. Suuure you did. Just like you forgot what you and he did last night?"

"Oh, yeah. I was totally thinking with my brain last night, for sure. Duh."

"Yeah, well, not that it would have mattered."

"What are you talking about?"

"I'm saying it wouldn't have mattered if he'd been staying on the other side of town. He still would have found you, whether he tried to or not. And nothing—

not even our heavy, locked doors—would have stopped him."

CHAPTER EIGHTEEN

Ethan

I WAITED IN my room until I heard them leave. I could just about kill Kiera for revealing our secrets after I'd worked so damn hard to keep it from Gabriel. The last thing I wanted was to scare the guy away, even though I knew I couldn't have a future with him.

Who'd ever want a man who has to

constantly battle with himself?

To fight the despicable duality that nature forced on him?

Nobody started a relationship with *that* guy. They might stick around if it developed long after they got together, but equally they might not.

How could I ever expect Gabriel to take on a relationship with a wolf shifter?

Especially so soon after learning we even exist.

After I'd shown him around town, I truly had wanted to escape from him. The man was a drug, and any time spent in his presence got my blood racing. Though he made my body strong and my cock hard as hell, all I felt when I was around him was utterly weak.

Even repeating the previous night's run had done me no good. As hard as I fought against it, the wolf inside had been starved for five long years. Ravenous didn't even begin to describe him.

As with the night before, I'd arrived back to a dark house. When I'd come in, skin soaked and pulse racing, I'd been utterly determined to head straight to bed.

I hadn't even made it as far as my room before the intoxicating musk of Gabriel called out and seized me by the balls.

And the fevered fuzz that had filled my head was unlike anything I'd felt with Clinton, or with any of my casual dalliances back in Chicago. The fire Gabe awoke within me utterly consumed my entire being. My heart, my soul, my lupine lunacy.

And it meant that in the light of day,

memories were almost impossible to isolate. Last night was nothing more than a cavalcade of carnal imagery. Hard muscle and slick skin, the aroma of perfection and the breathy song of ecstasy.

All I could recall for certain was that I'd gone in naked, had poured myself into that gorgeous human, body and soul... and then awoken with his delectable body tucked against me in the most heavenly embrace.

But it was fear, pure and simple, that drove me to leave before he woke. And to do my damnedest to hide any trace I'd been there.

Had I stayed, I knew I'd dive headlong into that man, time and again, until I lost any sense of myself. Now that he knew my true nature, our dynamic would be challenging enough. But him being my fated mate would likely be more than his human body and mind could ever handle.

As I stood and dragged my clothes on, I glanced in the mirror and sneered at my reflection.

Be honest with yourself, asshole.

I sighed, resigning myself to a life of torture, either way. The smart thing to do would be to leave right now, put hundreds of miles between us. Live a life empty of emotion, filled with loneliness. Anything, so I could simply be human.

Because more than anything, Gabriel's hold on me left me in abject terror; that he would drag my wolf back from beyond the grave.

And that I'd let him, thereby undoing all these years of effort.

All the best moments in my youth had

been as a wolf, yet they were shrouded—suffocated—by that one day of hell.

I knew without a doubt that Gabriel would fill me like nobody else could. He would complete me. But for him to have that chance meant I'd have to complete myself first.

To be wolf again.

I had to break it off with him, before someone ended up hurt.

Or worse.

CHAPTER NINETEEN

Gabriel

AS I SAVAGED my steak, I listened to my bestie relate the story of Ethan's life, as much as it could be told. It was the weirdest thing how I'd barely even met the guy—you really couldn't count the sex— yet, I had an insatiable hunger to know everything about him.

"So, you're telling me he was a little

furry monster all the time?"

Kiera nodded. "Pretty much. Any time he didn't have to be human, he shifted. He was a loner for the most part, but not so much by choice."

"What do you mean?"

Kiera shrugged, but her expression turned dark. "Wolves have what you might call poor color vision. A lot of them only ever see things in black and white. Ethan didn't fit in the way most wolves do."

"Because he's gay?"

She screwed up her mouth and crinkled her nose, as animated as ever. "A little bit. Stoke Ridge was a pretty backward place back then. It's only now that we're all part of Gray Vale that things are catching up with the rest of the world."

My heart raced in my chest. I'd kinda known the same struggle, of course. My parents had been cool with my sexuality. I think they knew long before I did. But most of my extended family were assholes about it.

"Also," Kiera continued. "You wouldn't believe it, but he was small. For a long time. A real late bloomer, that one."

"You're right. I don't believe it."

"Not to mention he's scary smart, too, obviously. The other kids gave him hell any time he used so much as a three-syllable word. And he had no interest in team sports, which of course meant, in their words, that he was some kind of fag."

"Well, hurtful words aside, it's not like they were wrong."

"Yeah, but it's like they got the right

answer with all the wrong working out. They didn't realize he was gay, because he wasn't even sure. They just tossed what they thought of as the worst insult in the world at him. The fucking dicks."

She looked off into the middle distance. "God, he loved to run, though. Not to hunt, really, though he did his fair share. And when he was older, there was some, uh... chasing of tails, shall we say?"

I got the distinct impression my friend was sounding me out. Testing me for jealousy. Hell, Latino blood was hotter than most, and the thought of anyone else even looking at my man usually got my claws out at the speed of light. Somehow, none of it seemed to matter this time around.

Because he is not your man, doofus.

He's just a guy you fucked, first with

your eyes, and then with your body.

"Hey, I never expected him to be a virgin. He might be a total prick, but uh... he's, like, not super-ugly or anything." That was the understatement of the millennium.

"This is true."

"So why isn't he still going wild? Living life, y'know... off the leash."

"Har-de-har. Well, there was one thing. He always had a little trouble shifting back."

I took a sip of my wine. "Really? You made it look so easy."

With a shrug, Kiera glanced around the restaurant. "Mostly it is. For some, it can be a struggle. Kind of like insomnia. You know, when you absolutely have to sleep, and that makes you stress yourself out so hard that you can't? It's like that.

The more you know you have to shift, the farther away it seems to move."

"And Ethan has that?"

"As a kid, it didn't seem to matter. He was happier as a wolf. It was just…"

"What? Come on, you can't dangle a *just* in front of me and then pull it away."

Kiera sighed and nodded. "Okay. You're right. See, it became a thing. He was already an outsider, like I said. Once the other kids found out, they used to pick on him about it. Like it somehow made him less of a wolf."

"So that's it? That's what made him turn away from it?"

"No, not just that. It's a long story." Kiera took another sip of her wine and then screwed up her nose. "Okay, it's not all that long, it just doesn't feel right me telling it. It has to come from Ethan. But one thing you really need to know is, he was mated before."

"Like, married? Yeah, you said something about it before."

Kiera shrugged and moved her head side to side. "It's a little bit like that. But it's a wolf thing."

"You keep saying that like it could mean anything to me."

Kiera suddenly turned serious. "Gabes, you gotta understand... I keep saying it because this is wolf country. There are bear shifters, too, and some other creatures that'd really stew your mind. But here, in both the Ridge and the Vale, it's all about the wolves. So, yeah, everything around here pretty much is a wolf thing." She rested her hands on top of mine. "And if you want to know Ethan, you're gonna have to allow for that."

With a sigh, I turned my hands over and squeezed my friend's. "What was his name? Ethan's mate."

Kiera paused as if it was a hard question. Finally, she seemed to resign herself to answering.

"Clinton."

"And he was like you guys? A wolf shifter?"

"Yeah, of course. But please, don't ask me to explain it all, okay? I'll just mess it all up. I know the facts but not the truth."

"Okay. I get it."

And I did get it. I had no chance with the guy. It really was as simple as that. It didn't make me jealous in the slightest that he'd been married, or mated, or whatever. Nor the fact that, no matter how he felt about this Clinton guy now, once upon a time he'd have to have been crazy for him.

Feelings change.

People change.

Hearts change.

No, for me, it boiled down to one annoyingly uncomplicated fact: he'd found pure happiness with a fellow wolf. There was no way I could compete with that. I could learn every last piece of truth and trivia about Ethan and his kind. But I couldn't ever belong.

Kiera squeezed my hands back. "Aw. Why so glum?"

"I guess I'm scared. Actually, it's more like terrified."

"Of what?"

"Of how stupidly hard I'm crushing on Ethan. And, oh, my god, how quickly. It's so new to me, and so weird, and I know it can't ever work. I'll never fit in around here."

"And why should you? Ethan doesn't."

"In his life, then. Okay, he doesn't love being a wolf, but it's still there. I'll never have that in common with him. And maybe he's not with Clinton anymore, but he clearly holds a strong place in Ethan's heart. I don't... I'm not strong enough to carry that kind of baggage for him."

Kiera looked as if someone had kicked her puppy. She leaned back, taking her hands with her. "Gabes, please don't push me for details. Let me just say Ethan and Clinton were happy, but they were not in love."

"How the hell does that even work?"

"Wolves, remember?"

"Latino, remember? Nosy as hell with habanero blood. Explain!"

Kiera made a point of taking a long,

slow sip of her wine, keeping her gaze locked on mine as she did so, apparently taking great pleasure in milking the moment for all it was worth.

"There's a process. I won't bore you with the details, but it's quite common to have couples who mate for life as wolves without ever feeling the same way as humans do. You know, that overpowering charge that you get when you're with the one?"

"The one?"

"Your fated mate."

For a moment, all I could think of was Ethan.

The fierce blades of his eyes.

The frightening heat of his cock.

Overpowering charge might very well be the exact way to describe how it felt when I first saw him.

And whenever he touched me.

Oh, and when he'd come into my room and taken me to heaven as easily as spilling a drink.

But it sounded so much like a fairy tale, I was prepared to write it all off as exactly that. Or at least scratch at the idea to find out its weaknesses. "How do you really know if you've found them, though? This so-called fated mate?"

The smile that crossed Kiera's face was fleeting, but so genuine it lit her up. "If they're wolves, then both partners know it right away. And pretty much every wolf around them can scent it." She reached across again and tapped me on the end of the nose. "Like I did at the party, the moment you and Ethan saw each other."

I could feel my cheeks heating up. "Oh." I put my hands up to cover the blush, but it was too late.

About two days too late.

If what Kiera said was true, then everyone at the party must have known how I felt. Everyone including Ethan, which must have been why he'd come into my room and fucked me so hard and so well.

And why I'd let him without even a moment's fight.

"So, if it's true, and I'm meant to be with him, then why he is being so hard to get along with? Half the time he's an arrogant jerk, the rest of the time he's shutting me out. Was Clinton so important to him he can't move on?"

Kiera pursed her lips. "Gabes, I'll say it one more time, and that's it. It's not my tale to tell. I mean, your average guy is a closed book most of the time anyway.

Present company excepted, of course. But dear cousin Ethan is all sealed up, and wrapped in duct tape. In a locked safe. At the bottom of the ocean."

"Ugh, I get it."

"Seriously, though. You're gonna have to get it straight from him, or else not at all."

"Huh. Not at all is not an option."

"Gabes? Tread carefully, okay?"

CHAPTER TWENTY

Gabriel

I COULD BARELY remember the rest of the meal, or our walk back to the house. My mind had been on Ethan, and what his secret—or secrets—might be. Though Kiera had tried to keep the conversation flowing at first, in the end she'd given up.

At the front door to the house, Kiera softly held my arm, making me wait.

"Gabes, remember what I said, huh?" Kiera squeezed my arm before turning and walking toward her car.

"Hey, you sure you don't want to be here, too, Kiera? Protect me from the big bad wolf?"

Slipping into her car, Kiera smiled while she shook her head. "I'm not even sure you want to be here for this. But I know you have a rock-hard head and you won't let this thing go, so..." She shrugged and closed the door, starting her car on the second attempt.

I crept inside, taking off my shoes as I made my way up the hall. At my bedroom door, I looked inside and paused, thinking on all of Kiera's warnings. It sure would be simpler to just pretend nothing had happened, and go back to my old life of singing to nobody. But that also meant having nobody.

Yep, it sure would be simple. But it would be anything but easy.

Instead, I turned to look back up the hall. And almost jumped out of my skin, seeing Ethan standing there, with a cold fire lighting his eyes and a wild cast to his smile.

"Why don't you ever shift?" I blurted it out before I even thought about it. "You're a wolf, too, right? Like Kiera?"

His nod was so small and quick it was almost impossible to see. "She's my cousin. It's a family curse."

"Curse? Apparently, everyone else loves it."

He prowled forward, the steel in his eyes flashing a warning at me. "Everyone but me, city boy. I mean, it's ridiculous. Such primitive behavior; howling at the moon, chasing bunnies, sniffing each other all over." He curled his top lip as he stopped right before me. "Be thankful you're only human."

"Hey! Watch what you say about my kind, mister."

"I meant in the sense that human is the only creature you are. You don't need to process the world through two sets of senses. You don't need to reconcile the animal within. Suppress that mindless beast." A small shudder ran through him.

"You, sir, don't get to speak for me. Yeah, okay, I'm human and nothing else. But that doesn't mean it's all simple and clean for me, either."

His laughter dug into my skin like a bee sting. "Please, Gabe."

I grabbed his shirt and pulled down, standing on my tiptoes as I did, just to get closer to his face. "You ever been human? I mean *only* human?"

"Unfortunately not."

"Then you don't know, do you?"

Gradually, the anger in his eyes cooled, and he quirked his lips into what looked like a genuine smile.

"All right. You have me there, Gabe." He worked his shirt out of my grip, straightening it when he'd freed it.

"So?"

Raising one eyebrow, he fired a fresh smirk at me. "So?"

"So why are you the only wolf ever to hate being a wolf?"

"I'm sorry, I don't know where you got the idea that would be any of your business."

I grabbed a hearty handful of Ethan's cock, through his pants, noting it was fully hard. "Maybe it was when you got this business all up in my business."

There was no mistaking the look of surprised pleasure that washed across his face. I made the most of it, seeking out the thick head of him with my thumb and rubbing just below it. The low hum that oozed from his throat made my cock all thick and pulsing with need yet again.

"So tell me, big guy. Why do you hate being a shifter?"

His breath grew shallower with every pass of my thumb. With his eyes closed, he reached across and curled his hand around the back of my neck. It seemed as much about holding himself upright as holding me close. When he finally spoke it was ragged, more gravel than hum.

"I... can't..."

"Can't? Or won't?"

Ethan shuddered all over, as if his legs were going to give out on him. Finally, he growled—a full-throated grumble of sound—and grasped my hand, wrenching it away from his package.

"Does it matter? I know you don't have the senses of a wolf, but surely even your pitiful human ones can tell this is beyond painful for me."

I couldn't help but recoil from his anger, though I didn't feel the slightest physical threat from him. I even managed to let his scornful words about human senses fall by the wayside. Because what I could tell without question was that, no matter what his words said, he clearly did want to tell me.

To unburden himself.

With tiny steps, I closed the gap between us, reaching for him as I moved.

His eyes flashed at me with some kind of heat. It could have been anger, but I was willing to bet—my life, maybe—that it was arousal.

When I slid my hands up his arms, he jumped at my touch, like he wasn't even aware I'd moved.

"Ethan, you can trust me."

He pressed his lips together so hard they formed a white line. Eventually, he relaxed them enough to squeeze out a few words. "I know I can, Gabe. It's myself I can't trust."

I figured if I wanted him to bare his soul to me, I had to offer up something to entice him. So I worked my shirt open and shrugged it off, my heart leaping with pleasure at the hunger that lit in his beautiful hard eyes.

Going for broke, I kicked off my shoes,

opened my jeans and let them drop. I stood before this beautiful demigod wearing nothing but my tighty whities.

I hooked my fingers into his thick hair and pulled. "Open up to me, Ethan." I used all my weight to pull his mouth down to mine for a soft kiss.

For a moment, he held firm. Then, with a sweet and scary growl, he took my request literally, parting his lips and devouring my mouth. I'd wanted truth and honesty from him. I'd expected it to come in the form of words, but it was there in every moan he uttered, and every caress he blessed me with. And I would never turn my back on it.

Except to let him take me from behind again.

Ethan slid his mouth down to my throat and the entire heat of his body seemed concentrated in that one spot. I threw my arms around his neck for fear of either flying away or simply melting. His breath coursed down over my chest like a waterfall of lust.

"Yesss." I'd meant to yell it but it came out more as a whisper, with a moan chaser. I fisted his thick hair and sliced a speedy hiss from deep inside his chest. He returned the favor by spearing his fingers into my hair and tightening, right at the top of my neck. With a rapid tug, he brought my scalp to life, kinking my head right back until I could feel his eyes and his mouth and his breath over every pore of my throat.

I leapt up into his arms, needing to wrap my legs around him. Not for safety, and not for balance. Simply to pull him closer, grind his body against mine, exactly where I needed him. The bristling, needy heat of my cock needed some strong treatment.

Like, right fucking now.

I locked my ankles around his ass and ground my raging boner up against the huge hardness of his cock.

"Come on, big guy. Let go."

I could have simply thought the words and he'd probably have heard them with those crazy wolf senses. But the moment I spoke, he tightened up again.

"Ethan, please. I'm so hard. I need you inside me."

"No, no... I can't."

"Don't you fucking dare, you asshole. We're fated mates, whatever the hell that means. I think it means you have to fuck me whenever I say."

He sank his teeth so deep into my

neck I wasn't sure if he'd meant to turn me to jelly or turn me away. But when he tried to pull my legs apart and drop me to the floor, I found a little of the wild animal inside myself, taking the back of his shirt in my fists and holding on like it was the last enchilada in the world.

"If you turn me down now, mister, they will be finding parts of you in the woods for decades."

"Gabriel, I'm warning you. You don't know what you're asking." He tried again to detach my thighs from around his waist. When that failed, he moved his hands up to my shoulders and pushed me into the wall, trying to get me off him.

I released my hold on Ethan's shirt and instead drove my short, sharp nails hard into his back, dragging them like claws over his shoulders, really digging in through the fabric. The big man stiffened and hauled in the sharpest breath I'd ever heard, even turning his face to the ceiling as if he was about to howl.

Everything slowed, at least in my head. Ethan brought his face back down to mine, the silver of his eyes nudging that little bit closer to blue. But it was his mouth that had me mesmerized... and terrified.

He had his top lip curled up as if it were a creature in its own right, the brilliant white of his teeth glinting through like a predator stalking me.

The room seemed to tilt, and tingles of sensation ran through my body, focused on every point of contact between us. It was as if Ethan was vibrating at a speed the human eye couldn't see.

And for the first time, I wondered if

maybe—just maybe—I should have listened to him and backed off.

There was something, like another presence in the room. A sound I could feel more than hear. And it was all over my body, from my neck down to my desperate aching cock. It was a sound too low for my standard old human ears to hear.

It took a moment before I realized what it was.

Ethan was growling.

Oh, god.

It was like a diesel engine vibrating against me. I still couldn't make out any sound, but where his thick cock pressed against mine, the sensation was unbelievable. And that was through layers of fabric.

I ran my fingers over his shoulders and beneath his arms, bringing them together again around his waist. Whether he was losing control or just desperate to get closer to me, I couldn't tell, but he ground his chest against mine, forcing my backbone into the cold wall behind me.

I knew it was a heavy moment. One that could tip the scales either way.

Intense erotic pleasure, or utter rejection.

But I wasn't about to back down just because Ethan literally had the strength to tear me apart.

I ran my clawed fingers gently up his back and hooked them around his shoulders, lifting myself to where my hard shaft could press on the tip of his cock. If only we were naked, the moment would be just about perfect.

As I lowered myself against him, I ran my hands back down. Without warning, I dug them deep into his back again, harder than before. I couldn't be sure, but it felt as if I'd managed to draw a little blood, even through his shirt.

Ethan's inaudible growl became a snarl of pain. The whole world spun like a carousel on cocaine as he dragged me away from the wall. He dug deep into the flesh of my thighs with his long fingers, gliding his hands higher with every rushed step he took.

By the time we arrived at the sofa, he had my underwear in his grip. And when he'd finished tossing me unceremoniously onto the cool leather cushions, he still had them in his grip.

Only now it was just shredded fabric.

I barely had time to even contemplate the shock and pleasure of being stripped bare in under five seconds.

And so brutishly.

"I fucking warned you, little one..."

Barely had he bitten out the words than he landed on his knees.

Between mine.

For a moment he drew in short, punching breaths through his nose, making random movements with his head.

Oh, god... he was scenting me.

Like prey.

He seemed to lose control of his eyes for a second before he curled his top lip up in that weird sexy scary grin he had. I held my breath, completely unsure if I was in any danger.

Ethan hauled my leg up to his mouth and bit into the soft skin on the inside of my knee, pulling a hot moan from my throat. He salved that little sore spot with his tongue and worked his way up my leg, biting and sucking, drawing closer to my raging hard cock with every kiss he planted.

I expected a tease. A little hover, maybe a cool breath, or even the classic move of switching to my other leg and repeating his actions. What I never expected was for him to open his mouth so damn wide, and to drive his mouth all the way down me with a power and a hunger like I'd never felt before.

I yelped—an actual high-pitched yelp— as he closed his mouth around me and hummed, scratching his hands up the length of my thighs. Every sensation my body could conjure, he pulled them inward, centering them on my most sensitive flesh, as if he'd given my balls some kind of internal gravity.

My hands seemed to be affected as well. I could have sworn I never told them to move, yet there they were, clamped around the back of Ethan's head, fisting his hair, holding on for dear life as he pumped his hot mouth up and down my length. I squeezed harder every time he sucked hard on my tip, and I released only when he did.

The swabbing of Ethan's velvet tongue around my fat head hit me like tequila, and his tight grip around my balls burned like lime and salt. His attention forced me to feel everything around me—everything in the world, it seemed—so strongly and so sharply I wondered if my body might not have room to hold the sensations. And when he slid one hand beneath my ass and bent me upward, pulling me as close to his mouth as he could get me, I almost lost myself completely.

The first tingles of climax crept through me, but before they'd even begun to gather properly, a new sound came into being. Two parts chainsaw, three parts dinosaur. If not for the nirvana of Ethan's mouth on my cock, I might just have fled for my life.

I knew right away it was his predatory growl again, only this time I could actually hear it. Soft and throaty, as old as time itself. The wolf within him was jostling for prime position. Even the flesh beneath his skin seemed to ripple, a tsunami of lust trying to find an exit.

I locked my gaze on Ethan's. The sheer depth of need shining from within him was beyond perfection. I'd felt wanted before, but only ever for brief moments, and only for parts of myself. Nobody had ever wanted everything I had... everything I was.

Never once had I felt so desired.

So integral.

Ethan turned his head and swabbed my shaft with his mouth, covering every single point of pleasure. Every pore, every vein, every tender millimeter. Even from my viewpoint I could see the glistening of his hunger all over my length, and even out to my thighs.

When he curled his top lip up even further and dug his teeth into my sac, I whimpered with want.

But when he shoved my knees up and slid lower, roughly pulling my cheeks apart, I swore I was about to have an out-of-body experience. He fired his tongue in against my puckered back door and tickled with the tip of it, making me quiver all the way through my body.

I gripped my own knees to free up Ethan's hands, and he snarled in appreciation. At least, I guessed that was it, because he swept those big paws of his straight down and gripped my ass cheeks, lifting me higher and spreading me wider.

The wet heat of his tongue gushed against my ass hole, wetting me completely. My balls trembled and my cock tingled with ecstasy as my wild man devoured me.

Stroke after stroke, he heated my hole, going deeper with every long lash of his tongue. I swore his tongue grew wider, fatter, with every passing second, and couldn't help but wonder if he was partway shifted.

Only thing I knew for sure was, I didn't care. Nobody had ever ignited such pleasure inside me.

When Ethan took my cock in his fist, and drove two fingers up inside my ass, I dragged in a deep, sharp breath from the pure surprising bliss and cried out in need. He pumped his hands in harmony and then hauled my balls into his mouth, rolling his tongue over and around each one, suckling even as my balls pulled up tight.

Suddenly, an enormous firework of ecstasy erupted inside me, sparking out through every nerve ending and racing up my spine. My voice seemed to take on a life of its own, pouring out of me in a keening moan of pleasure, and it seemed destined not to end until I'd emptied my lungs, and my soul.

Ethan let my balls slip out of his mouth with the most delicious wet smacking sound. As my climax crested, he opened up and embraced my cock in his savage mouth, growling with hunger as I filled it.

As the rich aftershocks of orgasm sent my body jittering, Ethan bounced his head up and down as he drained every drop from me.

When I'd finished, he came up off the end of me and narrowed his eyes, the silver orbs radiating pure ravenous desire.

Then he stood, tearing his shirt from his body like it was made from tissues. His sensual grace shone through in every movement as I studied the hard lines of his body.

The shriek of his zipper sent a fresh mix of fear and desire through me. It was like a clawed hand being dragged down my spine, hard enough to hurt in that way I loved so fucking much.

The rustle of his jeans falling to the floor brought a fresh ripple of nervousness to my skin, but the fierce strength of his hands had a settling effect.

He let some of my juice drizzle from his lips and onto his fingers, then coated my ass with it, gliding two digits inside me again with a smooth, erotic grace. I closed my eyes and arched my back as he made me slick and ready.

He let the rest of my come fall into his palm and stroked himself with a tight fist, coating his ferocious hard-on.

When he nudged that broad head in against my open, willing ass, I held my breath. I knew it was gonna hurt as he stretched me, but I looked forward to that burn in the most pleasurable way.

Ethan's voice had shifted away from

human and toward wolf, coming out in a low snarl that had me simultaneously more scared and more aroused than any one man should be allowed.

He captured me in the glowing silver heat of his eyes for a moment, and I nodded, following up by pretty much begging him to fuck me.

With a quick driving jab of his hips, he plunged half his gorgeous manhood up inside me, and I cried out like fresh-struck prey. Ethan drew back and bunched up his muscles, punching forward once more and this time his hips slammed into me. I had all of him inside, felt so stretched and full, and it hurt so beautifully I thought I might pass out.

My big, ravenous lover swooped his arms around me, lifting me like a damn puppy and carrying me in his embrace, and on the stake of his cock, through to the guest room. At the bed, he placed me down gently, slanted his mouth over mine, and kissed me hard.

He kept his momentum going, rolling over me and onto his back. Effortlessly, he pulled me up on top of him and gripped me at my hip and my neck.

I pressed myself down on the thick heat of his cock as I fought against the beautiful tears in my eyes. It was more than the intense, burning ecstasy of agony. It was the fierce, relentless connection that fired between us, that eschewed words or definition.

With his fat brute deep inside me, I hissed in pleasured pain as he squeezed my flesh, dragging all my thoughts and feelings down to where it counted. The bliss of his cock fired off salutes of ecstasy inside me, and the hardness of his chest gave me a perfect surface to press on while I bounced myself on him.

I dared not look him in the eyes anymore, knowing what power they already held over me. And the easiest way to avoid seeing them was to dive down on him and suck his tongue back into my mouth.

The man was everything, and everywhere. With his big hands on my hips, and his thick cock inside me. With his hot mouth on mine and his fiery skin beneath me. Not for the first time, I wondered if I truly was a big enough man to take this ride.

But when he started growling again, even more beastly than before, I suddenly had no doubt. He raised his hips from the bed, leaving me feeling weightless for a second, and hooked his clawed fingers over my shoulders. I shrugged, trying to wrestle control back, but he was too fucking strong.

He found my nipple with his teeth and bit hard into the stiff nub. He pulled down on my shoulders, driving my ass against his hard thighs and filling me so sweetly it was like a thousand desserts at once.

What an idiot I'd been to think I could have any control where Ethan was concerned. My mind barely completed that thought before the forked bolts of sheer ecstasy fired through my body again, driven on by the passionate roar of the climaxing man beneath me as he painted my walls with his scorching essence and I clamped down around his length, welcoming the heat of his release.

The pulsing of Ethan's hips eased, and

I drifted down to him like a dropped feather, landing softly, my mouth covering his. The heat of his skin toasted mine, and the shared sheen of sweat-slicked bodies made it so easy for me to glide down beside him.

CHAPTER TWENTY-ONE

Ethan

AFTERSHOCKS OF PURE pleasure kept firing through my mind and body. Bursts of sensation, mild spasms, tiny cramps... it was so similar to the onset of a shift that it only increased my belief that this man was some kind of home for me. Not that I could afford to entertain such fanciful notions as home.

Or even happiness.

Damn this sexy singer and his undiluted desirability. Damn his tan brown skin, his expressive eyes, his sensual mouth. Most of all, damn the way his lean, hard body called to my wolf.

I simply couldn't get enough of Gabriel. He was already an addiction. And to stay with him, to keep this whatever-it-was alive, would be nothing less than substance abuse.

"You okay, Ethan?"

His voice was syrupy with fatigue. All that did was make him even more desirable.

"I'm okay."

"Can't sleep?" He nuzzled at my chest, which only served to work him deeper into my heart, into my blood.

I already knew he was my fated mate.

Did he have to keep getting more and more desirable?

Fucking adorable, even?

"I rarely find sleep easily."

Gabriel ran his fingers through the hair on my chest and raised his head. "You think maybe it's because you have a whole other being inside you, howling to come out?"

"No." I found Gabriel's deep dark eyes with my own, and sighed. "Probably."

"Then why won't you free him? It won't scare me."

"You can't know that, Gabe."

He kissed my chest and worked his way up to my throat. "You're right, butt-face. I can't. But I believe it. And I trust you... Ethan."

It wasn't the first time he'd used my name. But it was the first time he'd said it like that. Like it was worth saying.

I closed my eyes, hoping it would stem the tears I felt forming. I'd worked long and hard to keep any man from trusting me like that. Only to find now it was the one thing I'd always needed.

Gabriel laid his head back down on my chest, and glided his warm thigh up over my waist. He was a delightful solid weight on me, hardness coated in silk. He held me in place, taking on my heat, and molding to my form. Grounding me like nothing and no one ever had.

And then he sang.

Soft and smoky, as smooth as bourbon. Some lullaby or folk song. The words were nowhere near as potent as the sound, or the fact the song was for me alone.

In the beauty of his voice, I understood

I truly had found a home. A solace I'd never believed in. The woman who'd spawned me had never been one for lullabies. By the time Abigail Larson filled the maternal role, I'd been too old and too jaded for kids' songs.

But in that moment, Gabriel enveloped me. In body, in scent, and in sound. He was in my heart already. And with his song, suddenly he bloomed in my mind, in parts I'd considered long dead.

I kissed his forehead lightly. Before I'd even finished, the sound of Gabe's voice faded.

And I slept.

***

I had my teeth in the throat of a lost black sheep. Tearing, choking, savaging. The rich delicacy of blood. Heat, scent, taste.

Somehow the poor creature managed to bleat, even with its neck mostly severed.

A second passed and the bleating morphed into the ring of my cell phone, pulling me from the first lupine dream I'd had in ages.

The fresh and spicy scent of Gabriel coursed through my body as I eased his delicious weight off my chest. As he stirred, a soft, sleepy moan escaped him and I considered crushing the phone in my fist just so I could taste him again.

When I checked the number, I almost went through with that thought.

"Hello, mother."

"Son, we need you. Your father's heart... please, come over at once."

"You're at home?"

"Yes."

"I'll be right there."

I gazed down at the hottie beside me, wishing more than anything I could stay. My craving was bone deep, and even knowing my father was in danger couldn't completely push aside the hunger. My cock was hard again, just from the heat of his skin, the scent of his hair. My guts ached, exactly the way they used to in puberty when I went too long without coming. Only this time, I knew, it wasn't my balls calling for release. It was my wolf desperately trying to chew through. To take control of me, for just as long as it took.

"No."

That was the danger I'd faced before, and I simply could not afford to go through it again. As much as I'd tried to deny it, my wolf was more than just part of me. We weren't merely two sides of the same coin. We ran in each other's veins. And if I let the wolf out now, it would never truly release me again.

Addicts who quit and then relapsed always felt it the hardest.

I had to end it with Gabriel. Though it would sap every iota of joy from my life, the mere fact I was still sitting there, captive to his body and the sensations he awoke within me, was proof my wolf could not be trusted. I was supposed to be rushing to my father's aid.

It was as painful as ripping out hairs, but I slid myself away from Gabriel and started dressing. Though I worked quietly, the newly formed bond between us struck again, and he stirred.

"Hey, handsome. What's happening?"

"Medical emergency. My father."

"Oh, no." He pushed the blankets off

his naked body and my damn wolf howled within. Gabriel awoke a protective instinct in me that no man ever had. He was not a small man, nor even soft. It was the softness and care in the man's eyes that had me struggling to breathe. And every passing second made me more desperate to dive back into him.

I turned away before my wolf could betray my human side. "So I, uh… have to go."

"I'm coming with you."

"Please, Gabriel. Don't push it."

"Hey, someone needs to have your back. And so what if they don't like me?"

I turned back, needing to ram my next point home like a nail. "They don't like me. They hate you."

The shock and pain on Gabriel's face was a scar I feared I'd never heal from. To know my words had cut him so badly was simply the worst feeling I'd ever had. Bar none.

"How could they? And how could you just blurt that out?"

"Honestly, it's not personal, Gabe. They hate almost everyone. The reason they only dislike me is that I'm their legacy."

"Well, nobody tells me what to do. I'm still coming with you."

I struggled for breath. My heart seemed to swell three sizes with the depth of my feelings for Gabriel. His courage, his determination and his sheer bloody-minded tenacity.

God, he'd be the perfect wolf.

While I was lost in his beauty, he slipped off the bed and pulled some clothes on. "All right, butt-face. Let's go."

"No."

"A straight out no? You're actually trying that on a diva like me?"

"I actually am. This is wolf business, little one."

Though he hadn't seemed to mind that pet name before, it had him bristling before me, narrowing his eyes and loading his pointing finger to shoot me in the face. "Don't you shut me out, dog-breath. If we're supposed to be fated mates and all that shit, then your damn parents need to get with the program."

I made a show of crossing my arms, of shielding my heart from him. My wolf whined at me to take him, while my human strove desperately not to be cowed. "Listen. You don't get to come into my life one day and then tell me how to run it the next. Understand?"

My heightened senses told me the slap was coming, but I let it land. His instinct clearly was to punch me, but something—love?—made him hold back.

I knew I deserved it, and a thousand more. Gabe landed another from the other side, his eyes brimming with tears.

"Bastard!"

The pain in his heart was an agony in my soul, but there was nothing else I could do. If I enslaved myself to emotion, I'd be entirely useless as a surgeon. All those years of education and training would amount to no more. I had to rely on all that clinical calm now. To excise this relationship before it took me over.

"Better you know that now than later, Gabriel." I blocked the next blow, which was far closer to a closed-fist one, and Gabe deflated before me, falling to his knees.

It wasn't until I'd walked out of the room that I heard him start swearing. And it took the greatest strength I'd ever known to stop from turning back and begging forgiveness.

CHAPTER TWENTY-TWO

Ethan

IT WOULD HAVE been quicker to drive to my parents' house, but without a car I had little choice. Besides, I didn't trust myself behind the wheel at that moment. The way my vision kept blurring was more than a nuisance. It would make me a hazard to everyone on the road. I tried to convince myself the tears were due to nothing more than haze in the air from the not-so-distant brush fires.

So, instead of driving, I ran, drawing on the stamina of the beast within, while striving to keep the wolf itself at bay. Oh, how my mother would be pleased to see me arrive on four legs instead of two.

Once again, I was faced with the quandary of my own duality. Shift into wolf form and I'd make it there in no time, but always with the risk I'd be stuck that way. So, I stayed with human form, even knowing it would take a few minutes more.

I arrived barely out of breath, and stormed inside. My mother greeted me in the hallway.

"You're here. Thank goodness."

"Where's father?"

Hugh called out from the living room.

"In here, son."

I raced up the hall and through the wide doorway. To find my father sitting in his favorite chair, a tumbler of gin and tonic in his hand and a pretty blonde standing beside him.

And I realized instantly what a fool I'd been. This was Clinton all over again.

Only worse.

Olga spoke from behind. "Now, son. Don't be angry."

The moment she said that, anger was the only emotion I could feel.

How could I have let them manipulate me so easily?

"Son," said Hugh. "This is Anthea. She's from quite good stock. The Milford Grove Pack. You know them? They're a few counties away, but still worth knowing."

Anthea herself smiled thinly at me. She showed no reaction to being talked about like a prize breeding sow. Nor did she appear to have any feelings for me at all. What was undeniable, though, was the way her scent simply drifted past me, without any effect.

I turned away from her to face my mother. "It's bad enough you don't trust me with anything. Now you think you can fucking convert me? You morons."

Olga caught her breath as though she'd never been so insulted in her life. A detail I knew only too well to be false, since I'd called them far worse before I left town last time.

Hugh stood, his own anger vibrating through his body. "Ethan. You will not speak to us that way. Especially in front of guests."

"I will, actually. You do understand that just because you are wolf doesn't mean you're obligated to cry it, right?"

"We had to get you away from that... human."

My anger instantly turned cold, and sat heavily in my chest. As it drizzled lower I could feel my other half inside me. The first tingles of a shift crept along the length of my bones, feeding on my rage. It was clear my parents could sense it as well, given the avarice in their eyes.

"Good, son," Hugh said, with a smile. "At least use your anger for something. Find your wolf."

It took all my strength simply to hold the shift in check. I couldn't completely suppress it, but at least for the moment I could stop it going any further. The truth was, I desperately wanted to give it free reign, and doubted my ability to resist.

My mother stepped around in front of me again. "Release your true self, son. You don't really have to mate with Anthea. We can find you an even better one. Come home."

The horror show of my own family hit me like a slap. I couldn't imagine how Anthea must be feeling at that moment. But if she was wolf, she'd surely have picked up from my scent and my bearing that she was not... my type.

I realized suddenly that she'd only ever been a pawn. The fact she was female was not a desperate attempt to convert me. It was only ever intended to enrage me, by making me think that.

Suddenly, the image of Gabriel flashed into my mind. The irresistible splendor of his naked body, and the ragged ache I felt knowing I'd likely just thrown away any chance I had to be with him.

But then I recalled the way he'd stood, and dressed, more than ready to come with me. Despite being outnumbered and outgunned, he'd been prepared to confront these fools on their home turf. These people I could barely believe I shared blood with.

He'd been ready to put his head almost literally in the wolf's jaws.

Just for me.

All my life, my parents had sung the praises of our kind. Espousing their belief that wolves were superior to all other beings. That humans were weak, feckless and foolish.

In a matter of seconds, Gabriel had proved them utterly wrong. He, a mere human, had displayed far greater strength of character than either of my parents ever had.

He was only human... but I knew now for certain; in his heart, he was wolf.

The more I thought about him, the more it eased my tension. Oh, my beast was still prowling down there, hungry for blood. But where I'd usually force him down, compress him, this time I didn't need to.

Gabriel had brought me balance like I'd never felt. In only a matter of days, he'd crashed through barriers I'd imposed on myself. He'd coaxed the darkness up into the light, and somehow, it worked.

Fuck, it bloomed.

Having my mate in my life would mean I wouldn't have to fear the wolf. More than that, though, I just might be able to embrace him.

I closed my eyes and let Gabriel's strength wash through me. If I was the luckiest man on Earth then I might have a chance to win back his heart. But I had to leave right away.

Slowly, I opened my eyes again. "Anthea, it's very nice to have almost met you, and I'm sorry you were lured here on false premises. Please, let your pack know this was the work of Olga and Hugh Roddick, and nobody else. My leaving now is nothing to do with you."

Before the girl could even get a word out, I spun on the spot and marched out. My mother followed, yapping her displeasure all the way, but I barely even registered a syllable of it. My one focus was getting back to Gabriel.

Before I lost him forever.

CHAPTER TWENTY-THREE

Gabriel

I'D TRIED MY damnedest to follow him. When Ethan ran out, I'd scrambled to my feet and followed as closely as I could. With those stupidly long legs of his, and his... I don't know, wolf cardio classes, I'd had no chance. And I ended up barefoot, shaking, and coming down with an anxiety attack, in the middle of a town I didn't know at all.

"Mister Mendoza?"

I tried to calm my breathing as I turned, finding Abigail and Bernard Larson standing before me, arm in arm.

"What's happened, darling?" Abigail reached out and took my hand in both of hers.

"Your nephew is a…" I wanted to call him all kinds of names, but I'd fallen so damn hard for him the words just wouldn't come. All I wanted was for him to come back. Just because I wasn't a wolf didn't mean I had no instincts, and the world had never felt more right than when I was in that man's embrace.

"Oh, Ethan. Well, that's not so bad." Abigail let a sigh escape her. "Kiera tells us she's brought you up to speed on the town, and its people. Is that right?"

"Uh-huh."

"Then I can tell you, we've been hearing reports of rogues. I thought you might have encountered one."

"Rogues?"

"Rogue shifters. Possibly bears. It's probably nothing, darling."

Bernard lightly touched my shoulder. "Come with us, please? Tell us everything over a coffee. Our treat."

It was a short walk to the café, and we took a table on the sidewalk.

"So, Gabriel," Abigail began. "What seems to be the trouble?"

"Ethan. It's always Ethan. My life was perfect and then he came along and turned it inside out."

Bernard patted the back of my hand, the same way my own father used to. "I know it's not directly our business, but the way our daughter tells it, your life seemed a long way from perfect."

"You're right. It's not your business." I suddenly realized what I'd said. To the people who'd been kind enough to let me stay with them for the weekend. "Oh. I'm so sorry. I didn't mean to be rude. I'm just messed up."

"It's all right, Gabriel," said Abigail. "You must understand, Ethan is the son we never had. I'm sure you're aware by now that you are, without a doubt, his fated mate. Yes?"

"That's what they tell me. Fat lot of good that does."

Their coffees arrived, breaking through the conversation for a moment. Bernard took a sip of his and then turned to me again.

"Now, I don't know the detail here. But

let me tell you what I do know. Ethan is a man who's still in pain. I take it you don't yet know the details, but I assure you, he's holding on to something very dark. And a lot of that is inextricably tied to my damn sister and her husband."

"Yeah, well, that's where he is right now. I mean, I get it. His father's sick or something, and Ethan's a doctor. I get that he had to rush over there. But what he didn't have to do was treat me like a piece of shit on his shoe."

Bernard and his wife exchanged a look, and then Abigail spoke.

"Darling, we've just come from their place. Hugh is not sick in the slightest. Nor in need of any medical attention. In fact, he was busy lecturing that live-in student... oh, no."

Bernard bounced his fist on the table.

"Those assholes. They're at it again."

My head spun at the rapid change in their mood. "What? What's happened?"

"It seems my sister and her husband are playing their old games with Ethan's life. Trying to mate him with a wolf."

"What? And he just ran off to do it?"

Abigail shook her head. "Never, darling. You said he was called over to tend to his father?"

"That's what he said. I was asleep when he took the call. If there even was a call."

"Ethan is the most honest man we know, darling. And even if he were capable of lying, you're the last person on earth he'd try it with."

I felt like flipping the table in frustration. "Then what the hell is going on? What happened to him and Clinton?"

Bernard sat back and shook his head. "I'm sorry, Gabriel. I'm sure you've heard this plenty of times already but it's not our story to tell. You're really going to have to get that from Ethan himself. Just promise me you won't make any permanent decision until he opens up. Okay?"

"He never will."

"He will, Gabriel, if you ask him. He'll open up completely. At least, if he knows what's good for him, he will."

"Yeah? Well, he ran from me to be with his parents, so he clearly doesn't know what's good for him."

Abigail smiled, though there were a few icicles hanging from it. "You're technically an orphan, darling? Kiera told us."

"Yes. My parents were killed in a plane crash when I was seventeen."

"And you'd give anything to see them again?"

"What does this have to—"

"Why do you think it should be any different for Ethan? He's lived the last five years of his life as though his parents were gone. If they've tricked him into believing his father truly is at death's door, it's no wonder he ran over there. Medicine is his calling in life, and those two have never supported it, let alone embraced it. He finally had the chance to show them he's not the waste they've always told him he was."

I glanced across the street, only to see the man himself, running back toward the Larsons' house. If anything, he was moving faster than when he'd left.

I made to yell out to him, but Abigail grabbed my arm. "Not here, Gabriel. It needs to be done in private. Pin him down and get the truth. His truth."

I hesitated for a few seconds. No way could I risk tossing my heart to that man. Not if he couldn't break the shackles of his destructive family. The pressure would tear us apart and I'd be left shredded on the floor somewhere.

Maybe literally.

Bernard rested his hand on my shoulder. "Go to him, Gabriel. But remember what I said. Hear him out, and then decide. Please."

The short walk back over to the Larsons' place did nothing to clear my head.

Why the hell couldn't this man be open with me?

He wanted me as much as I wanted him. I didn't need any of those stupid wolf senses to know that. It had hung thick in the air like humidity every time we were within a hundred feet of each other. Yet there was no denying how hard he'd tried to push me away.

More than once.

The house's front door bore the brunt of my seething mood. I slammed it so forcefully behind me it probably deafened any wolves in the area.

I charged up the hall to Ethan's door and thumped everything I could against it—hands, feet, elbows, knees—demanding he open up.

First the door, then his heart.

"Hey, you big tool. Let me in."

Ethan had clearly moved in silence, like a damn wolf. The door came open just as I'd lined up a swift shoulder charge, and I ended up landing on the floor right in front of him.

"Gabriel. I thought I'd lost you."

I looked up, ready to rip him a new one, when I was silenced by the one thing I never expected.

Tears on his cheeks.

As I regained my feet, I pointed up into his face. "Yeah well, who says you haven't, butt-face? I need to know everything. About Clinton and your parents and... and just everything." I'd been warned to tread carefully, but this was too important.

And too close to my heart.

Ethan put his hands over his face. "I've tried so hard to put it in the past, Gabriel."

"Well, you've sucked at that. Whatever the problem is, you carry it around your neck in everything you do." I pushed him backward, hoping to get him all riled up. That seemed to be the surest way to get him speaking honestly. "I know what your stupid parents were up to. Don't ask me how, I just know."

Ethan sighed and hooked his hands around the back of his neck. "I didn't think I could despise them any more than I already did. And then they prove me wrong."

I resisted the urge to snuggle up against him. As much as we both might need it, I needed the truth even more. "I'm not going to stand between you and your family. And I'm not going to force you to make a choice. Your folks can't stand that I'm human, so screw them. But I promise you, I am not going to be with half a man. A man who won't be true to himself."

"Take care, little one. Take great care."

"Ha. I'm not about to start now, butt-face. This is it. Your last chance. I can see it's burning a hole through you. I know you need to tell me everything. And I need you to open up to me, or I swear I'm gonna—"

Ethan moved like the perfect predator, taking my mouth with his and subduing me in an instant. Cutting off my air, and the flow of blood to my brain. As his tongue swept across my lips, my head grew light and fluffy, while my body turned to hot fudge. He had his palm against my throat, his other hand cradling my head as he mashed his lips against mine, suckling at me like I was nectar.

I'd been so determined to draw his pain out of him so I could heal it. To truly know this man, in every way.

Now, with the taste of his mouth, the smell of his hair, the touch of his skin, suddenly, I only existed through him, through the ways he filled my senses. Gravity failed me as he swept me up into his arms and slammed me back against the wall, driving from me the last iota of breath I'd managed to hold.

It took more strength than I'd ever known, but I broke the kiss and forced my way out of his embrace. "No, Ethan. I can't... it's not fair."

"What's not fair?"

"I can't help myself here. I am this close to sinking myself completely into you. One hundred percent. But you're holding something back from me. And it might be small, but it's clearly heavy. If we fall into bed again now, I'll never be able to get over you."

"I don't want you to ever get over me. I need you like water."

I pressed my hands in against his heart, but my only intention was to keep him from swallowing me whole. I dredged my voice up from the molasses of lust inside myself.

"Then you know what to do."

CHAPTER TWENTY-FOUR

Ethan

I LOOKED OUT of my bedroom window. The fires over the hill were kicking out a lot of smoke, but so far there hadn't been any call to evacuate. Not that I'd mind a whole hell of a lot if that were to happen. It was hard enough to be back in Stoke Ridge with all the memories it held for me. But to be surrounded by all these shifters as well was doing my head in.

And now this guy, this perfect temptation, was cutting at me like a fellow surgeon. Asking me to eviscerate myself of all my feelings and my faults.

And God help me, he was right.

I did want to.

I needed to, in fact. I'd kept it pressed down so hard it had fermented. If anyone deserved to know my full story, it was Gabriel. For us to have our future, he needed to know my past.

Fated mates were so damn inconvenient.

I turned back to him, where he sat on the bed, his eyes awash with love and his body trembling in anticipation. He looked so much like prey it awoke my wolf once again, and it took me an enormous effort to push that feeling back down.

Every time I was in his presence, he tugged at my beastly side without apparently doing anything at all.

The sexy bastard.

I took a seat on the floor, lowering myself before him in adoration. "This is not an easy truth."

"I know that much. Kiera and her parents all warned me. But I really need to know you."

I nodded and studied my hands a moment. "All right, then."

And as I spoke, I closed my eyes, traveling back in time. Revisiting the scents and the sounds much more than the sights.

The rumble of thunder came closer as Clinton stripped off, racing ahead of me. The damp earth and humus filled my nostrils when that cute smile lit up his face; the smile that only came when he was about to shift. I fell to the ground, feet tangled in my jeans, the scents of a thousand prey animals firing into my brain.

Then the momentary pain and exquisite pleasure of shifting.

Clinton ran ahead of me, his tail dancing and beckoning. I nipped at him, mock hunting until a prey animal might cross our paths.

Rain was coming. The smell was everywhere. Lighting and thunder filled the night, making everything more urgent. More fun.

A deer startled off to the right, and we turned in pursuit. These were the times we were at our best. Most compatible.

Clint flushed a doe from the bushes and we paced it, one on either side.

Hunting for fun, not for food. Wolf time was everything.

Heaven.

Our hearts trilled as we ran. I felt his pulse as clearly as my own.

The rain hit so hard. Got harder. The world was nothing but scents.

Rich soil, dead leaves, rabbits, water.

Rain hitting us harder.

Harder still.

Lightning.

Clint took cover under a tree and I came in behind, pressing against him to take the rain. To shield my mate.

The wind blew faster, the storm grew fiercer. A bright flash as lightning hit the tree above, thunder sounding at the same time. A branch fell, and before we could run, it landed.

Clint yelped, and even through my

layers of wolf, I knew right away he was hurt badly.

I pulled at the thick branch, but even wolf jaws couldn't move it, couldn't break it. Clint shifted, his whimpers becoming screams. He should have stayed wolf. All the shift did was tear his belly to pieces as wolf turned to human.

Blood.

Clint's blood.

All my world ran red.

He needed my mind. He needed my hands. I had to shift.

Shift.

Must shift.

There, it was almost in reach.

Shift.

Shift!

Clint's breath slowed as his eyes drifted closed. I slowed my breathing, *searching inside myself for the answer. For the man I had to be.*

I came back to the present, to the house. To the man before me.

My fated mate.

Gabriel's face glistened with shed tears. "What happened?"

I stared at my hands, studying them. Burning their form and their function into my mind. How I could have used those hands back then, to lift the branch. To staunch the blood, to carry him to safety.

I pressed my fingers to my mouth. The mouth I could have used back then to form the words. To tell Clint not to shift. To let his wolf take the pain. To let the branch block the flow of blood, rather than have it gouge away at his morphing body.

And finally, I admitted my pain. The

pain I'd never put into words before. Not for Kiera, not for Clinton's family. Not for anyone.

Until now.

"He died. With my head on his chest, his gaze holding mine until he closed his eyes forever. His hand squeezing my paw, and me unable to squeeze back. Unable to shift back."

Gabriel slipped off the bed and knelt before me, resting his head on my thigh.

I sighed as I stroked his beautiful hair. "That day, I lost my love."

"He must have been amazing."

"He was, but that's not what I mean. Clinton was a wonderful man, and an amazing friend. We were mated, true enough; but we never once felt anything for each other like what is right here..." I put my hand to my chest. "Between you and me."

I screwed up my face, but couldn't stop tears from rising into my eyes. "My best friend died. But I lost so much more. He took with him all the love I'd ever had for my wolf. I knew then I couldn't trust the beast."

"But he's part of you. Half of you."

"And what happens the next time I'm stranded without hands, without words? Whose life will be ended then? Because it could be yours, Gabriel, and I will never stand for that."

"Oh, baby."

I tensed beneath him, unsure if I was truly ready for the weight of all this. For understanding and sympathy and—dare I believe it—*love.*

Gabriel curled his arms around my calf and looked up into my eyes. "I'm so sorry, Ethan. I didn't know." As if he could sense the turmoil inside me, he released his grip and stood. "I shouldn't have pushed. I should have listened to everyone."

Before I registered what was happening, he'd turned and walked away. But he didn't even make it halfway across the room before I'd caught up, seized his arm and spun him back to face me.

"Where do you think you're going?"

"Baby, I'm sorry. I didn't mean to hurt you. The way people talked, it was like you had a messy divorce or something." He swallowed heavily before speaking again. "You have so much to deal with. I... I was thinking about myself, and what I want." He tried to drag his arm away, but I wouldn't release him.

"And what about what I want,

Gabriel?" I grasped his other arm and pulled him against my hard chest.

"W–what do you want, Ethan?"

I ran my hand up the side of his face, combing it through his hair on the way back down. Though I followed the movement with my gaze, I quickly turned my focus back to his. "A week ago, there was only one answer to that. Right now, there is still only one answer." I kissed his forehead lightly. "But those two answers could not be any more different. Before, I wanted solitude. Now... I want everything."

"Oh, everything. Is that all?" The little kink in the corner of his mouth awoke that ancient hunger. The one that relied on senses, not words. The hunger I was already learning to embrace again.

I could never truly be mated to this

man, in the purest sense, without my wolf. And I struggled to believe I could live another day in the world without being mated to him.

I cradled his head, and bent to him, caressing his lips with mine. Soaking up every scent of his sexy body, every tiny sound of his voice.

By kissing him like that, by taking his essence into my blood, I'd finally set my wolf free. Though I could sense its caution, feel it waiting to be chased back into the darkness, I knew without a trace of a doubt I needed my beast as much as my human form. The two were one, and could never be divided.

"What do I want, Gabriel? I want you. Forever. And I... I want my wolf back."

The scent of tears all over his cheeks was both a rich temptation and a sharp knife. As I carried him to my bed, I kept my gaze locked on his.

I knew I was lost in him. He was my life now. And through him, my wolf had re-awoken.

CHAPTER TWENTY-FIVE

Gabriel

ETHAN TOSSED ME bodily onto the bed, as if I weighed no more than a pillow. In seconds, he'd torn every shred of clothing from my body, his hunger becoming a physical force. He stripped his own clothes off just as quickly, and filled the room with a low, fierce growl.

He leapt over me and held me down in

that way I'd never grow tired of. The way that made me feel secure, rather than trapped.

His beautiful eyes darkened for a moment as he scanned my naked body.

Every freckle, every pore, every scar.

I'd never been so proud of my own body, because I'd never had anyone look at it the way he did. Not like I was perfect, but like I was *everything*.

"You're mine, Gabriel. I can't even try to deny it anymore. I knew it—and my wolf knew it—the moment I caught your scent."

He wasn't saying anything new, but there was a sense of ceremony about it. As if it was a spell and he had to say the words just the right way.

"I am yours, Ethan. But only if you're mine."

"I am only yours, little one." He curled his top lip up to reveal his teeth. And the way they'd grown just that little bit longer and sharper. The wolf staking its claim on him.

And very soon, on me.

I nodded. Words simply wouldn't work at that moment.

He closed his eyes and simply breathed. "You will be my mate for all time." His voice was barely a whisper, yet it reached me like a roar.

Ethan dipped his head and seized my mouth in a kiss that was as much hunger as lust. He slid his mouth across and took my earlobe between his teeth, working his way slowly south down the hot skin of my neck.

The lower he moved, the more ferocious he became. By the time he was at my hip, the man had given way to the beast. Not so much in form as in nature.

And somehow, it was as exhilarating as it was terrifying. Just to know I could inspire such passion in this man.

Ethan drove his mouth down my cock, snarling with ravenous desire as he worked me higher and higher. In what felt like only a few seconds, his blistering attack had my consciousness swaying, and my climax boiling up.

I found the strength to push him backward. I curled my legs up and swung them past Ethan's face, rolling onto my belly, raising my ass from the bed and presenting myself to my conqueror.

Every hot-blooded, sweat-slicked, desperate inch of myself.

Ethan's moan grew deeper and rougher, until it was his wolf growling through his human throat. He fell upon me, driving his tongue against my hole with all the power and barbarity of the wolf inside him. He worked me so hard, so fast, and I'd never been more open to another person. I gripped my ass and opened myself up to him, willing him to take me any and every way he wanted.

Ethan sank his teeth into my skin, and all I could do was whimper with the twinned pleasures of fear and arousal. He snarled, his deep voice vibrating through me and making my balls physically tingle.

My big brute released me for a moment and fled to the bathroom, coming back with a bottle of lube. He snapped it open and poured the cold oil onto my puckered hole, and I swore the stuff must have turned to steam. I was that hot.

The slick sound of him lubing up his

own thick cock only made me more ready for him. I wasn't fully warmed up, I wasn't sure I could take him again so soon... but I wasn't prepared to wait.

When he snared my hips with his hands, the sharpness of his nails was obvious, like they'd shifted a little closer to claws. Everything about his presence thrilled me, and even more so when I could sense his beast just below the surface.

He nudged his broad head in against my ass, and paused. I couldn't read his mind, exactly, but I knew why he'd stopped. Making sure I was okay.

"Do it, Ethan. Set your wolf free." I glanced back up over my shoulder. "Go wild."

He drove forward and filled me in a heartbeat, stretching me so hard, so quickly, that it was the most perfect blend of pain and pleasure.

"Your skin is immaculate, little one." Ethan sounded trapped between man and beast. As if he was striving to keep the civilized human in control, while inevitably the wolf gnawed its way out. It was the hottest thing I'd ever heard.

And when he snared my hair in his fist and pulled my top half up off the bed, it brought my skin to life. I tingled from scalp to toes, not just from his touch, but from the way I sensed his eyes scouring every pore of my body.

With every drive of his hips, he sent wild sensations clawing their way up my spine, until my head was a bird's nest of pleasure. I was losing myself already, becoming, in my mind, nothing more than an extension of Ethan. I was more at home here, in his bed, in his embrace, than I'd been anywhere else in the world.

He released my hair and clawed both hands around me. One over my heart, the other over my cock, manhandling me so beautifully as his nails dug in to my skin and created a whole new burn. I lost control of my spine and fell forward out of his grip, landing face down on the bed. Only the strength of my lover kept my ass in the air.

"Little one..." Ethan rasped out the words. And then there was nothing but heavy panting and thick growling as he leaned down on me, angling that magnificent cock so it filled me in the most perfect way, nailing my sweet spot with every thrust.

The weight of his body rested on his hands, flat on my shoulder blades, and my breathing became both the ultimate luxury, and totally meaningless. Surely, while he ignited my body like that, I needed nothing else to live. No food, no water, no breath.

Just Ethan's goddamn perfect cock.

The spiraling fingers of bliss within my balls picked up speed until they became a maelstrom, and as Ethan punched his hips against my ass, I saw a white light behind my eyes. His weight grew too much and it forced my knees apart. I came down, flat on my belly. He stayed inside me as his body slammed down on my back.

His beautiful deep voice cracked as he roared with ultimate pleasure, and a bloom of piercing heat ignited my shoulder blade.

My whole world suddenly exploded in

ecstasy and I cried out. Pleasure that seemed to form in my bones, and pierce my skin drew uncontrollable sobs from my body. This was a climax from another world, and bizarrely, it seemed to flow down from my shoulder to my balls and then race like fire back up my spine only to make the same fierce cycle once again.

Then, as Ethan reached his own climax deep inside me, my ass drank the heat from him and I tightened around his thickness with a long, loud scream as I let loose once more, my release coating the mattress beneath me. Only then did I realize he had his teeth embedded in the flesh of my shoulder, deep and hard, sharp as hell. The pain was pleasure and that pleasure was the world.

I was absolutely, unquestionably, his.

Forever.

CHAPTER TWENTY-SIX

Ethan

AS MY ORGASM subsided, I felt my mind struggling to return to my body. My last conscious memory was of Gabriel urging me on. Insisting I get as beastly as I could.

I caught my breath, the wolf side of my nature unwilling to step back from the brink. Though I'd already come, the uneasy balance between my two sides felt for all the world like the struggle to hold back an orgasm.

Beneath me, Gabriel's sweat-slicked body quivered with the aftershocks of his own climax. My senses whirled, my beast and human sides intertwined in a way I'd almost forgotten could happen.

I teetered on the edge of shifting, for the first time in years, reluctant to turn away from it too quickly. It wasn't unlike the sensation of dozing.

As my mind finally processed the sweet and salty tang of blood, I sighed against my tender mouthful of flesh.

And my humanity returned in a flash, like an icicle slicing through my heart. My teeth and nails, both slightly elongated, tucked back into their human form immediately, and I released Gabriel's shoulder from my bite.

"Oh, fuck," I said, my voice a harsh whisper in the near silence of the room.

"Mm. My sentiments exactly."

Oh, hell.

I shook my head, and licked over the open wound on Gabriel's back, speeding up the healing process.

"Hey, butt-face," he hummed, his voice quivering with pleasure at the touch of my tongue on his brand new wound. "That's enough of that. I couldn't possibly go again."

In seconds, the bleeding stopped, and his skin closed over, leaving behind only a scar.

My mark.

He didn't know.

How could he know?

Until this weekend, he hadn't even

known shifters existed. But what was done was done.

I screwed my eyes closed and came down beside him, holding him tight against my body as he drifted inevitably to sleep.

And in the morning, I'd have to tell him the truth. That my mark was much more than just a scar, and held more weight than a wedding ring or a contract. With that mark, he'd be just like me.

Wolf.

***

Even though I was highly experienced, in life and in lust, I had never felt anything like the beautiful ache of having Gabriel fall asleep in my embrace. And the potent surrender of waking up beside him.

As a surgeon, I'd grown used to

implicit trust. People who neither knew me nor liked me would routinely submit to my strengths, and place their lives in my care. It was the coldest and most clinical kind of trust I could imagine. And that suited me just fine, professionally.

I'd literally held dozens of hearts in my hands, yet not one of them had affected me like this. It was only a metaphor, but the way I now held Gabriel's heart meant everything.

He was my life.

My completion.

And I had absolutely no doubt how lucky I was to have found him. Not all wolf mates were in love. Hell, it was only through finding Gabriel that I realized how shallow my connection to Clinton had been. Mates in function only. Our wolves had been compatible enough not to kill each other.

Gabriel, though, filled my world and my senses like nothing ever had. My bond to him felt stronger than the immutable tie to my own wolf, if that were even possible.

But above all else, Gabriel had shown me the majesty of embracing my wolf again. And the folly of trying to deny such an essential part of my own being for so damn long.

Which turned my mind, jarringly, back to my mistake last night. I might be highly intelligent, but I was a fucking idiot. To think I could simply open my wolf's cage and expect him to play nice. That he might sit, beg, and roll over just because I said so.

After long years in the dark, in the wilderness, of course he had turned feral.

And the moment I gave him a glimpse of freedom, he had taken me over.

I ran my fingers over my mark on Gabriel's shoulder and he stirred, sighing lushly in his sleep. I pressed into it and his sigh caught a little friction and turned into a throaty moan.

As always, the sound of his voice, especially when expressing pleasure, spoke straight to my cock and I was rock hard in seconds.

"Damn you," I muttered, as if my erection would listen. Now was not the time. As much as I'd love to take him, yet again, he had to know the truth before anything else could happen.

There was a process, a ceremony to turning humans, not unlike a marriage. A tradition, that I'd unintentionally pushed aside.

In the throes of unstoppable passion, I'd lost control, and I'd turned the man I loved. I could only hope he'd understand, and forgive me. But I had to face facts; it just might have cost me any chance of a future with him.

CHAPTER TWENTY-SEVEN

Gabriel

IT FELT UTTERLY self-indulgent to be awoken by sunlight streaming through the window, instead of by an alarm. I couldn't remember when I'd felt more alive. Like I'd been plugged into a charger overnight and was ready to devour the day.

The feel of Ethan's hard body

snuggling in against mine was even more luxurious. The man was a human furnace. Wait… a half-human furnace.

I turned in his embrace, searching for those incredible silver eyes of his.

But when I found him, his expression was anything but happy.

"What's wrong, Ethan? Is it your parents?"

He shook his head, closing his eyes and somehow closing his face off to me as well. "I have to tell you something. I hope you won't hate me."

"Impossible. Unless you tell me you're married."

He flinched at that, and my belly tightened up. I slammed my hand into his shoulder and sat up. "Oh, for fuck's sake! You are married?"

"No, Gabriel."

I allowed my breathing to return to normal as I relaxed a little inside.

"Well, thank fuck for that. I really didn't feel like killing you today."

"I mean, I'm technically not. Not exactly. It's... it's us. You and me. We're mated."

"Well, we sure have done it enough times."

Ethan sat up, and I couldn't stop myself from admiring every damn inch of his perfect, hard body. I had to bite down on the desire rising within me, which was pretty damn weird, considering I was still pissed at him for scaring me like that.

"That's not quite what I mean."

What the hell was wrong with him?

So far, he'd been pretty clear with his communication. At least, once he'd opened up.

But now he couldn't find the words to tell me what was going on?

Surely we were past that by now.

"Look, Ethan. Whatever it is, we'll get through it. I can't believe I'm saying this so soon but... I'm stupidly in love with you, and I can see you feel the same way."

He finally opened his eyes again, and pressed his big, hot palm against my cheek.

"God, you're beautiful, Gabriel." He came forward, capturing my mouth with his and forcing me down onto my back. He kissed his way to my hard belly licking and nipping at my flesh, tracing every freckle and mark with his fingers. "Every damn inch of you."

The break in Ethan's voice as he praised me was even more magical than the words themselves.

Ethan's ravenous hunger for me went beyond everyone and everything I'd ever known. And as wonderful as that felt, it was also a little bit scary.

When he gripped my thighs and wrenched them apart, bowing as if to take my balls in his mouth again, I let out a long moan, which somehow rolled over itself until it became a growling sound.

What the hell?

Where did that come from?

The moment that beastly noise escaped me, it was as if someone had thrown cold water over Ethan. He sat bolt upright, shaking his head and turning his face toward the ceiling.

He let out a long, hard breath, and then relaxed back onto his knees.

"Gabriel... I fucked up."

"We all do. Even brilliant surgeons.

Cut yourself a break, Ethan."

"But it affects us. You."

"Now you're scaring me. What did you do?"

He looked down at his hands, and sighed heavily. "I lost control last night."

"And how. It was amazing."

"I gave you my mark. On your shoulder."

I frowned, and raised my hand, reaching over to the exact spot he'd sunk his teeth in. "Oh... yeah. I thought I might've dreamed that. Boy, you really went to town."

"You don't understand, Gabe. That's what I meant when I said we're mated. It's something I would've hoped to do sometime. Eventually. With your permission." He ran his hand back through his lush hair. "I didn't mean to, but I'm so out of practice with my wolf, and I... I couldn't stop him."

I closed my eyes as I glided my fingertips over the mark. It gave me little thrills, almost like squeezing my cock, though not as concentrated. A harder press sent pain signals that were still rich with pleasure racing through me.

"So," I moaned. "We're mated. I was already sold on you, in case you couldn't tell, you big galoot."

"It's so much more than that, little one."

"Why the hell can't you just come out and say it?"

He grimaced and slid off the bed, standing tall, but turned away from me as if in shame. "That mark? It's because I bit you. And it means... it means I've changed you."

"Is this some weird wolf crap?"

"Yes."

I grinned and slid my legs over the edge of the bed. "You and your damn kind are loco."

"Our kind."

"No, *your* kind. Wolves. You're barking mad, every one of you."

"That's what I'm telling you, Gabriel. That bite—my mark—means I've turned you. You're like me, now."

"I'm... I'm a wolf shifter, now?"

He turned back to me, eyes closed, defeat written all over his face... and nodded.

For a few moments, I stared at the wall. I stood, and stumbled around the room. "You're serious. Aren't you?"

"I am." He dropped to his knees and gazed up at me. "I don't have any excuse.

Only reasons. And it doesn't change the way I feel about you, except to make it stronger."

So, just like that, he'd ripped my life to shreds. Nothing would ever be the same. I let out a sharp, howling scream and stepped past him, running down the hallway to my own room.

I yanked my suitcase open and disemboweled it, searching for something—anything—to wear. I finally settled on a pair of jeans and a loose old t-shirt.

Ethan appeared in my doorway, clearly trying to block my way.

"Please, Gabe. Talk to me."

I turned and punched at his shoulder like a drunken washed up boxer. "Most guys can't keep it in their pants. You just couldn't keep it in your mouth, could you? Now you expect me to believe I'll grow fur and howl at the moon?"

"You will. You'll be magnificent. And it will be the most liberating and exciting experience of your—"

"This is the same shifting thing that you said was ridiculous, and primitive, and a curse on your life?"

His sigh was clearly disappointment more than frustration. "Okay, yes, I said all that, and more. But you know now why I felt that way."

"Yeah, I do. But I now also know you're a lunatic with no grounding in reality, otherwise you wouldn't be spinning me this crazy line of bullshit." I elbowed past him and headed for the front door.

"Gabriel, wait."

I spun quickly and put my hand into his face. "Talk to the paw, asshole."

HIS HEALING HEART

***

I ran out of the Larsons' house, slamming the door so hard I expected the window to break. I had no idea where I was going, nor why. There was simply a wordless voice firing through my head that impelled me to run. And a ridiculous strength and stamina flooding my body, unlike anything I'd ever known.

With no exact destination in mind, I let instinct take over, and it led me to Ethan's family home. I'd never been there, yet something—scent, inherited memory, psychosis—told me exactly who lived there. The bizarre voice inside became a beastly growl, telling me I should kick their door in, and confront the man's parents.

Instead, I simply stopped outside and

clenched my fists, letting the anger well up. They'd treated me like dirt, of course, but that was hardly the point. I was far angrier at the way they'd treated my man all through his life.

Wait... was he *my* man?

After that stunt he'd pulled last night with those fangs of his, it was so hard to tell what was what.

I barely understood this new force inside me. It was as if I'd developed a split personality, but one that had a physical presence rather than a mental one.

What was more frightening was that it was composed almost purely of appetites.

Hunger and need and rage and power.

My humanity cracked and fell away beneath the swelling of the wolf inside me, and I let it escape the only way I knew how.

Through the power of my voice.

It started as a low hum, but quickly gained strength. Within seconds it turned into a growl, and then a mighty scream of rage, directed at the Roddicks' house.

The drapes parted, and Olga's stony face showed, a cell phone held to her ear. The only words I could make out were *he's here.*

The beast within took more control of my body. I crouched, ready to pounce at Ethan's mom. Nothing could stop me— not the twenty feet of space between us, nor the double-glazed windows.

"Gabriel!"

Fuck.

Ethan.

Only that could stop me.

I turned to see him running up the street toward me, and I let out a howl of frustration, turning on the spot and sprinting away.

As I reached the corner, I glanced back, fearing Ethan would be right behind me. Thankfully, he was trapped with his mother, who'd come outside to stop him.

I followed the streets of Stoke Ridge for a while, and found myself at the candy store where Ethan had ended our tour before. Without a second thought, I simply ran on into the forest across the road.

The moment I entered the semi-darkness of the thick, lush vegetation, all the tension inside my mind simply eased. It was as though I'd come home, suddenly. And that had to be the wolf within me.

I hadn't planned any of this, of course. And even though the whole situation was overwhelming, I still didn't plan to run too far. This would have to be a bargain-basement pout. That life-altering jerk would just have to come running after me and apologize again immediately, rather than in an hour's time like most guys.

I slowed to a jog, and let myself adjust to the new force inside me. It wasn't all that different to having sex, in a way. This thing—this wolf—was so big, and I just had to ease myself around it. Find peace with it.

In all honesty, it wasn't like I was actually against the idea of being a shifter. It just would've been nice to have been asked.

Or to even be aware it was something that could happen, for fuck's sake.

My wolf senses elbowed the human ones aside. The forest was absolutely filled with scents, though most of them were muted by smoke from the distant brush fires.

Those fires weren't a danger, but the wind had brought both the smell and haze across to Stoke Ridge. I couldn't see clearly for more than fifty feet in any direction, and despite my anger, I still managed a thin vein of sensible thought.

I rounded a thick tree and leaned back on it, listening for Ethan's footsteps. Every man knew, whether he was gay or straight, human or shifter, it was his duty to follow and to apologize. Except those times he wasn't supposed to, of course.

Any second now I'd hear him.

Any.

Second.

Finally, the crack of a twig beneath a heavy foot sounded from the other side of the tree and I swung myself around, hands on hips. "Well, it's about time... ohh."

I had, of course, expected Ethan, maybe on his knees and looking forlorn. Maybe even with big fat tears in his steely-silver puppy dog eyes. What I hadn't expected, was the man mountain who was actually standing there, hands at his sides like a gunfighter, completely naked, and glaring at me like I was a fresh morsel, ready for the taking.

Close to seven feet tall, and with arms as thick as my legs, he was a giant of a creature. But it was the cold, predatory light in his eyes that gave me real pause.

In an instant, I knew he must be one of the rogue shifters folks had been yapping about. If size meant anything, then he unquestionably had to be a bear.

At least he was only one man, though. With the fresh feeling of strength pulsing through my veins, I was oddly confident I could get away from him.

Hell, he didn't have shoes on.

Or pants.

No way he'd be able to chase me through the thick underbrush without cutting up his feet. Or maybe dislocating his hip when that monster cock of his started swaying.

"Well now," he said, his voice deep and gravelly, with a strong redneck lilt to it. Even over the smoke of the distant fires, I could smell the harsh chemical tang of bourbon. "Lookie what we got here, Mike."

"Mm-mmm." Another voice, with the same raspy hint of danger in it, sounded from behind me, sending my heart into overdrive. "A li'l ol' lone wolf. What you doin' all the way out here on your lonesome, little man? Everyone knows wolves are pack animals. Why, one wolf on they own is 'bout as useful as a paper umbrella."

I dared not turn around, but the way the second man's heat washed over my back told me there was every chance he, too, was naked. I closed my eyes as that guy flicked at my ears and ruffled my hair, like a cat playing with a mouse. "So? Why you out here all on your lonesome, fur-ball?"

"Don't call me a fur-ball." Instinct told me I should keep my strengths secret. "I'm no wolf."

The big guy in front of me scratched at his head, the movement echoed in the jiggling of his thick, somehow threatening, penis. He moved his head around, sniffing and sneering. I could hear the other one, Mike, doing the same. He spoke first, again making me jump.

"What you got, Walt?"

"Fuck, I can't tell. Damn smoke. Can't smell anything else."

"Well, maybe you shoulda been more careful with them joints you were smokin' back there, dickwad. Half the fires are your fuckin' fault."

"Screw you." Captain Cockwobble stepped right up to me, so tall my vision was filled with just belly and chest. Until he ducked and sniffed again. "Yeah, I can't tell. You sure you ain't wolf?"

"I'm human, and proud of it."

The big one in front of me—Walt—stepped back, his eyes wide and his hands up as if I'd pulled out a gun. "Woah... you're human?"

"Uh-huh."

"Damn. Hear that, Mike?"

"Yeah."

Clint scratched his chin. "You know what scares us about humans, boy?"

"N–no."

Mike snaked his arm around my neck from behind, almost cutting off my air. "Not one single fuckin' thing."

Walt bent his face right down to mine, his hot, wet breath coating my skin. "Well now, if you're human, then you must be the one we're here lookin' for. Ain't ya? Roddick's little bitch boy."

"Screw you. I'm a fucking diva. You're the bitch boys."

"Yeah. You're the one, for sure. They said you'd be here in the forest."

"What the fuck? Who said? Who are you assholes?"

Mike tightened his arm around my throat, completely blocking my airway. He released it a moment later but the message was pretty clear. It was a demonstration of what he could do, if he wanted.

At first, panic overtook my brain. I tightened up, my pulse raced, and adrenaline had its way with me. It wouldn't have mattered if these guys were regular old humans; I'd still stand no chance against their strength.

Physical power was not my answer.

Maybe talk would do it.

"What did you mean, you were looking for me? I'm nobody."

"Shut it. A mouth like yours is only good for one thing."

Walt guffawed right into my face. "One thing at a time, anyways."

Mike dug his thumb into the center of my back. "And don't go thinkin' we won't just 'cause you're a guy."

Walt gave me a light slap on the face. "I ain't had any pussy in months. I'll take ass instead. Ain't too proud to fuckin' wreck you, bitch boy."

Okay, so clearly talk was useless, and against two men this huge, I didn't have the muscle to back up any fight I might start. So, I closed my eyes and centered myself as quickly as I could. All I really had was the possibility of surprise. These guys were strong as fuck but dulled by alcohol and weed.

I threw my arms upward and wrapped my hands around the back of Mike's neck. A split-second later, I hauled my feet off the ground.

The speedy shift of my weight worked

beautifully, pulling Mike down and forward. As I headed for the ground, I kicked my feet out, catching that big, flopping dick of Walt's right in its heart. As he bent double in pain, his head slammed into Mike's, and the two of them roared with pain.

Mike's grip around my throat loosened, and as I hit the ground, I rolled to the side, breaking free from the grip of that mighty arm, and scrambling to my feet.

"Ethan!"

I'd barely finished yelling his name when one of the bears clipped my foot, tripping me over. Knowing I was too far gone to save myself, I spun so I could land on my back and be ready for whatever came.

What came was a huge man I didn't recognize. Had to be Mike. I curled my legs back against my chest, ready to lash out. The big guy lumbered straight at me, like he knew for sure I couldn't hurt him that way. As he towered over my prone form I kicked at him, but he simply caught my feet and rolled me over onto my belly.

The impact knocked most of the breath from my lungs. The big asshole drove the rest of it out when he landed on my back.

His stinking breath poured over my shoulder, but rather than recoil, I spun my head toward the source of it, bringing my elbow up at the same time and slamming it into the side of his head, hard enough that he groaned and rolled off to the side.

Still fighting to fill my lungs, I clambered back to my feet. I couldn't call Ethan again until I had air to use, but I thought his name as hard as I possibly could.

Before I could run back toward the road, a massive hand grabbed me from behind, the thick fingers latching onto my t-shirt and yanking back, tearing it from my body.

"Little fuckin' bitch boy." It was Walt again. He got his fist in my hair and pulled so hard my feet slid out from under me, and I landed on my ass for the third time. I stared up into the ice of his eyes. He was bent over, still with his fist in my hair. "You fuckin' see how this is going down? Two of us, both bears. And you, just a lowly little human—"

"Wait, Walt." Mike had come up behind me. He seized me by the neck and bent me forward over my own legs. "Look at that."

He dug an elbow-sized finger into my shoulder. The one Ethan had marked.

Walt hissed. "You lyin' little queen. You said you was human. Fuck, they told us you was."

"I am." I swallowed my fear. "Wait, who told you?"

"It was—"

"Hey!" Walt cut right across his buddy. "It was Father fuckin' Christmas. Asked us to check you were still a naughty boy."

Damn.

Mike had been about to tell me.

"But why? What's in it for you?"

Walt pulled me up by the hair. "A thousand bucks buys a lot of hooch. And a lot of cooch. I'd rat on my own mother for half that."

I winced through the pain in my scalp. "Who the hell would pay you so little, just to attack me? What the hell have I done?"

"Bitch boy, I don't know and I don't care. 'Cause now it turns out you're a wolf, and the price just doubled."

"I keep telling you, I'm not a wolf." I couldn't tell anymore if I was trying to convince them... or myself.

"Then what the fuck is this? Huh?" As Mike barked out the words he twisted his fat finger in Ethan's bite mark, the bear shifter's rough skin and sharp nail biting into me. "That's the mark of a wolf."

"No, it's the mark of a psycho idiot who thinks stupid stuff happens."

Mike looked over at Walt. "It's still fresh. He's wolf, but he ain't never shifted."

"I keep telling you. I'm not a wolf. I just happened to fuck a guy who turns into one. He got a little toothy, that's all."

Mike roared with laughter. "You simple little turd. Don't you understand what that bite means? Like it or not, you're a fuckin' wolf now. Which is just gonna make this more fun."

"Yeah. I like prey what fights back." Walt rolled me onto my front and pulled my ass into the air. "They squeeze so fuckin' tight when they struggle."

I tried to lift myself off the ground, but Mike pushed down on my shoulders with all his hefty weight. As much as I wanted to fight, to escape, it was all I could do just to tug tiny breaths into my lungs.

The moment Walt's huge paws hooked into my jeans, I tightened up across my whole body. I tried to call out, in frustration, in fear, just a call for help, but there was barely enough air in my lungs to make a whimper.

No! No!

It sounded so loud in my head, but it wasn't even a whisper in my throat. The only sound was the shriek of stitches parting as Walt tore the denim of my jeans, ripping everything away and baring my ass.

Before I could make sense of the moment, Mike's weight suddenly shifted off my shoulders, and Walt swore loudly. When I raised my head, I saw the reason.

A huge, gray wolf.

And without ever having seen him in this form, I knew immediately who it was.

Ethan!

CHAPTER TWENTY-EIGHT

Ethan

I'D ALMOST HAD him, outside my parents' house. The link between my mate and me was ridiculously strong, despite being so new. It had called to me like a beacon.

And when Gabriel—my mate—turned and ran, I was ready to follow. As strong as he would be with his new wolf abilities,

I knew I was stronger and, more importantly, faster.

But as always, my mother had other ideas.

"Ethan, stop."

As she came down the front steps, I swore I could see a jaunty little skip in her step. She grabbed my arm before I could avoid her.

"Let me go, Olga." There was no way I'd ever call her mother again.

"Son, you're being completely irrational. Can't you see it's over?"

"Oh, it is, is it?" I flipped my arm out of her grip and rounded on her so quickly she stumbled backward. "So, how do you explain the fact he has my mark?"

"H–he what?"

"That's right, Olga. Last night, I made things official. He has my mark... because he's my mate." Somehow, the truth of it all became much more potent in that moment, and I simply couldn't wait any longer to chase Gabriel down and claim him back.

"Oh, no." Olga lifted her cell phone and hit redial, her hand shaking worse than I'd had ever seen it before. "This can't be."

More than anything, I wanted to let my wolf loose, and direct him straight at this woman before me. Instead, I let loose my disgust and rage on her cell phone, slapping it out of her grip and smashing it with my foot. "It is. And you can just get the fuck over it."

The momentary catharsis of inflicting damage was enough to satisfy my wolf's bloodlust, at least for the moment. My only focus now was to get to Gabriel, and do everything I could to make things right with him.

With all the smoke haze filling the forest, I couldn't track him, either with human eyes or wolf nose. So, I simply opened my mind and let it lead me.

In seconds, I had a good feel for my mate's presence. He wasn't far... but somehow, I knew he wasn't safe, either.

The moment I heard him call out my name, I leapt into action and sprinted toward the sound. My wolf growled within, but until I knew what I was up against, I resisted the urge to shift. I'd grown rusty with it after years of suppression and I already knew the worst thing in the world was to be stuck with paws when only hands would do.

I could really use the extra senses, though. The fires were nowhere near us, but the smell of smoke hung heavy in the air. It was possible Gabriel had simply sprained his ankle. But until I had him in my arms again, I couldn't trust that he'd ever be safe.

A deep ursine howl of pain off to my left gave me both a direction to head, and an urgent reason to sprint.

He was not alone.

He was not safe.

My mate needed me.

And though I fought it with every rushed breath, the memories that thought conjured were impossible to ignore.

I tore away my shirt as I ran, knowing my jeans would come loose by themselves. Lupine hips were far more slender than human.

I found him just as the huge guy flipped him over. The fact those two had even got him onto the ground sent a bolt of incendiary anger through my core.

They think they can touch my mate?

Hurt him?

Rusty be damned. That fiery rage fed my wolf and in seconds, I'd shifted. Just in time to see the big bear rip his clothing away.

For a moment, the world was stuck in molasses. Every second seemed to take a minute. I pushed my human into sleep mode and thrust my wolf right into the driver's seat. And it reminded me exactly what was so wonderful about the animal kingdom.

No reasoning.

No bargaining.

No fucking mercy.

The one with his filthy hands on Gabriel's shoulders was closer. I ran noiselessly and leapt straight at the bastard, taking him around the neck in a vise grip. There were no words strong enough to describe my anger, and no wolf would understand the language anyway.

I snarled as I speared my teeth into the tender skin. The guy bugged his eyes, clearly expecting death any second.

But despite my unhinged rage, I couldn't completely push my human side down. Especially that damn oath I'd taken about preserving life.

"Ethan!"

The dread in Gabriel's voice was everything. I released my mouthful and turned, just in time to duck away from the enormous hairy paw the other guy had swung at me.

Bear shifters.

With the smoke and my mate's peril, the scent had escaped me. And if these two were typical of their kind then I could, for once, sympathize with his parents' disgust.

With only a moment to spare, I raised my head and howled. We were a good distance from town, but there was always a chance someone would have their ears on. I at least had to try calling for help. When I finished, I locked my eyes on my mate's.

Run, Gabriel.

I thought it as hard as I could, even glancing off to the side, in the direction of the town. Hoping he'd get the hint. I knew I could buy him enough time so he could at least get to the road, but one wolf against two bears was never going to end in my favor. As long as I could save my mate, though, it would be more than worth it.

I ran straight at the big bear, ducking another wild swing and diving between the guy's hind legs. As I slid to a halt, I turned and drove my fangs into the back of my foe's thigh.

Already fighting for balance, the bear swiped at me, succeeding only in falling onto his side. By that time, the other one had shifted. He wasn't as big, but he was still plenty big enough. He dropped to all fours and ran at me, teeth bared and tongue flailing.

In desperation, I released the fallen guy's leg and ran forward again, right up the big, hairy back. I leapt over the top of the approaching bear, catching him by surprise. As I landed, the bear overbalanced and slammed heavily on his back, giving me a chance to get a little distance.

I'd made sure to move the action farther away from where Gabriel had been, so he could make his escape even better. What I hadn't expected was to see him still standing there, naked, a thick branch in his hands. He held it like a baseball bat and cocked it, ready to swing, every time one of the bears moved.

For a moment, I lost myself in the vision. My perfect mate, my hard-bodied, soulful singer, ready to take a losing fight all the way to its conclusion. And for the first time, I could admit to myself that this was beyond any kind of love I'd felt before. That this transcended simple compatibility of mind and deliciousness of scent. This was the kind of love that everyone assumed was lust. Because it hit fast, and it hit hard, and it was fucking eternal.

HIS HEALING HEART

I was pulled from my reverie by a different kind of hard hit. The boss bear had fought his way back to his feet and slammed his huge paw into my neck, knocking me half way across the clearing. When I struggled back upright, my guts clenched, seeing the massive beast charging straight at Gabriel. To my terror, I saw the other bear coming in from the side.

I snarled with pure venom, shooting forward, hoping to grab the big one before he could get his teeth or claws into my mate, but the blow to my neck made movement hard.

Like I'd been sedated.

My heart froze as both beasts stood, ready to fall onto Gabriel. And as hard as I ran, as desperate as I felt, I was powerless to stop it.

I expected the next sound to be Gabriel's flesh tearing, and his beautiful voice screaming. Instead, there was a thick sounding clunk, like a golf club striking a ball, only played at one-quarter speed. And when the big beast fell, it was not on top of Gabriel, but off to the side, taking out the other bear in a moment of sweet serendipity.

My heart filled with love and pride as I saw my sexy fighter still standing there, the branch in his hands now only a stub, the rest of it broken away from the powerful blow he'd delivered to the big bear's head.

It was only a moment of peace, though. That impact would have killed a man, but all it did was slow the bears down for a few seconds. I leapt forward and placed myself between the danger and my mate.

There was no chance I could beat them.

There was no way I'd give in.

I took a second to turn to Gabriel and whine at him, desperate for him to run back to town, to save himself. But either he didn't understand, or he was as stubborn as a tired bull. With all that hot Latin blood, I was more willing to believe the second.

"It's okay, Ethan."

I yapped sharply in reply.

No. Go.

"We got this, butt-face."

I could hear the fatigue in his voice, and took an extra second to lick his leg. He responded with a lightning fast scratch behind the ears.

And then he was falling to the side, a sharp yell of pain firing from his throat. I nuzzled in at his side, suddenly scenting fresh blood.

Gabriel had his hands pressed to his belly, where deep crimson fluid was gushing out.

No!

I turned and bared my fangs, but before I could even snarl, the smaller bear had his mouth on the back of my neck, and sank his teeth in. For all my strength, I was suddenly powerless. The bear stood, clenching his prize, as I writhed and fought to no avail.

The next sensation was a pile-driver punch to the belly, mixed with the cold agony of long claws spearing into my flesh. I yelped and froze, a tiny part of my human consciousness telling me not to make the damage worse by struggling.

Or shifting, like Clinton had.

The bear took the chance to pull his teeth from my neck, securing me instead with both front paws.

From the moment I'd heard Gabriel's first desperate cry, I had been prepared to give my life to save his. My own death, though, would mean nothing if he lost his life, too.

The bear grunted and shook, as though the earth was quaking beneath his feet. I bent my head back, hoping I could at least land a couple of bites and go down swinging.

But what I saw filled me with surprise and pride. There, on the bear's back, fisting its fur, was Gabriel. The bear shrugged as if trying to dislodge him, but he held on and clambered higher. A moment later, he had the bear's ear grasped in one hand, and with the other he raised a foot-long stick.

Not even the slightest hesitation showed in his face as he speared that stick into the bear's other ear, driving it deep into the canal and causing him to scream with agony and fling me away.

The moment of triumph ended almost as soon as it began. When I landed I looked back, only to see the bigger bear swipe at Gabriel, tearing deep lacerations into the flesh of his thigh and sending him thudding to the ground again.

His scream hurt me worse than any of the blows or puncture wounds. I clambered to my feet and limped across to my mate, standing over his traumatized form and growling up into the faces of both bears. I snapped at one, then the other, as they moved in for the kill.

CHAPTER TWENTY-NINE

Gabriel

I'D NEVER KNOWN pain like this. And not the physical damage I'd suffered. None of the ragged tears in my skin mattered at all. It was the agony of having found Ethan—found the man who ticked every damn box—only to immediately be facing death, lying on the floor of the forest, bleeding out. That hurt me more than every other heartbreak in my life combined.

The past few days had been a torture of emotions. The ones I hadn't wanted to feel, and the ones I'd never known I could.

Like a spicy meal, where the pain is pleasure.

My head was a helium balloon, and I could barely squeeze my hand closed over the deep wounds in my belly. The gashes on my legs were seeping blood, and I knew it was over. Ethan's belly ran with blood, too, yet he stood over me, fighting to his last breath.

I plowed my fingers into the fur on his back, my final desire to be skin-to-skin with my mate when my life ended.

As my vision dimmed, I lay back on the undergrowth and sighed. My face was wet, and I couldn't tell if it was blood or tears.

From one side at first, then seemingly all around me, I heard the light crackling of leaves underfoot. Then, in what felt like an explosion of sound, suddenly there were wolves standing beside me, over me. I opened my eyes and counted at least six of them, including Ethan. A pure black one, a pure white one, and a few combinations of the two. Their snarling became a roar, like machine gun fire, and it had the bears backing away rapidly.

I recognized Kiera in the mix, and then smiled as I let my head fall back to the ground. The bears were backed up against a couple of trees, and the six wolves—even the badly wounded Ethan—closed in for what I assumed would be the kill.

The bigger bear stood, looking around

himself, and then slipped around the wide tree trunk. The smaller bear went the other way, and the two of them loped off into the forest, each with three wolves on their stubby tails.

A moment passed while I lay still, waiting for the bliss of sleep, knowing I'd never wake from it. I looked up into the beautiful blue of the sky, and the patterning of green from the trees. The bears and wolves had moved far away, and my senses were dulled enough, that I felt nothing but peace.

Then my wolf filled my vision. Ethan lapped at my cheek, and fell beside me, partly on me, and whined at me like a lost puppy would. I scratched him behind the ears again and smiled, hoping he could see me.

I had a blue sky on a warm day. I had

a soft place to lie. I had the man-wolf I loved more than life itself wrapped around me.

With nothing left to do, I opened my mouth.

And I sang.

CHAPTER THIRTY

Ethan

I SOAKED UP the perfection of his scent. His skin filled my senses, his breath was beauty. I licked at his neck and he laughed, a sound made weak from trauma.

Then the rich copper scent of his blood hit me anew. The blood I'd only ever scented through his skin before, now leaking from his wounded body.

The seed of my human mind was buried deep under the skin of wolf senses. Gabe's wounds were severe, but unless I could shift, I couldn't tell how bad. And I certainly couldn't do anything for him without my hands.

If I licked his wounds I could help them close, but I could do nothing for the damage inside them. That would only make things worse.

I closed my eyes and pictured how I looked as a man. Tried to hold the image of myself from looking in the mirror. But just like when I tried to order myself to sleep, the harder I searched for my humanity, the deeper it hid.

Gabriel ran his fingers into my fur and scratched at me. A ball of anger filled my belly and chest, which only drove the man inside me further into the darkness.

Rage fed only my wolf; it starved my human.

My only solace was that there was every chance we'd die together. To lose my companion once had been hard enough. But if that bitch they called Fate killed my true mate, then I knew I'd die soon after. I would have no will to live.

Gabriel held me close, and to my surprise, he started singing. Just a light crooning, a sweet little melody made irresistible by the sexy rasping of his voice. It was so soft I doubted a regular human would hear it, but it was a symphony to my wolf ears.

I closed my eyes and lay my head on his chest, letting the music of his song and his body fill me. My rage at the unfairness of life eased away from me, and I slowed my breathing, ready for whatever came after.

I took comfort from the sensation of Gabriel still moving beneath me. The cool of the ground against my skin. The soft feel of my mate's nails, scratching against the smooth skin of my back.

I sat bolt upright as the truth hit me. Gabriel's voice had worked its magic again.

I'd shifted without even realizing.

"Gabe!" I patted his face and he stirred, looking up at me through half-closed eyes.

"Hey there, butt-face. Thought I'd never see you again."

"Wait here a second."

"Please?" The edge of panic in his voice nearly sliced me in two. "Don't leave me."

"If I don't, you'll die."

"And if you do?"

"You might not."

He swallowed, and a fresh stream of tears ran from his eyes. "Then stay. Let me die in your arms."

"No!" I didn't mean to scare him, but he had to understand how vital it was. "I will be back in ten seconds."

I pried his hand loose from my hair and ran as quickly as my wounds allowed, back to where his cast-off jeans had landed. Wadding them up as I ran, I made it back to his side and pressed the bundle to his belly.

"I'm so sorry, Gabe. This is going to hurt like hell."

I hooked my arms under his frame and lifted him, pressing the wadded jeans into the lacerations on my own belly, and held him hard against myself, trying to staunch both wounds in one hit.

Gabriel winced, but didn't cry out, filling me with a fresh burst of pride for my sexy warrior.

My wounds were almost as bad as his, but there was no thought of rest or recovery. My only stop on the journey back to town was to gather up my shirt and tie it across Gabriel's thigh wound.

I kept walking, one foot after the other, maintaining only a vague sense of time passing. My consciousness threatened to fade time and time again. It was only when I wandered onto the road in front of a passing car that I realized I'd reached the town.

I was too dazed to even register the identity of the driver, but thankfully, whoever it was had no problem helping out. Together, we bundled Gabriel across the back seat. The driver grabbed her cell phone and called ahead to the hospital.

I slid in beside my mate, cradling his head as I grasped his hand. "Hold on, Gabe. This will be a rough ride."

CHAPTER THIRTY-ONE

Gabriel

HE WAS RIGHT. It was a hell of a drive back to town. I kept drifting lower, toward the blackness of sleep, only to be pulled back into some form of consciousness by Ethan asking me questions.

"Gabe, what's your blood type?"

"Uh..."

"Please, baby."

My mouth felt like socks. Not the cute little toe socks in the pretty colors. More kind of, like, the ones where you had a little bobble thing up around the heel. I maybe still had a pair of those back home for when I felt like being whimsical and more of a diva than usual. Something like a canary yellow, or a peach. But no, actually, my mouth didn't feel like those socks. More like a basketball player with athlete's—

"Gabriel. Stay with me."

"Hunh?"

"Your blood type?"

"Uh... A positive?"

"Are you asking me or telling me?"

"Sweet. Thanks."

A minute later, or maybe an hour, we came to a screeching halt. I heard his voice, and a couple of others, but they were speaking in some weird language, and it was all buzzing and hissing. Maybe I'd been kidnapped by aliens.

Hell, if there were shifters, why couldn't there be aliens?

The car door opened and a hundred hands grabbed me, hauling me from the back seat. I seemed to be flying for a moment before landing on a skinny little bed. A bed that rolled. The sky was falling. Or maybe just moving. Then lights and darkness and lights and darkness and...

Nothing.

CHAPTER THIRTY-TWO

Ethan

I CAME OUT of my anesthesia haze, looking around the hospital ward. I prodded weakly at the thick bandaging on my belly, satisfied everything was up to my standard.

It took me a moment to realize Kiera was there, sitting beside my bed. She smiled when she noticed I was awake.

"Hey, you big lump."

"Killa."

She stood and kissed my forehead. "We thought we might lose you."

Suddenly, my memory cleared. Watching my mate being taken into surgery, and being unable to control any part of it, had been an absolute torture. I recalled how my rage had threatened to overtake me again, and if not for my own urgent need for medical attention, I might have shifted. Just to process the fierceness of my anger.

"Gabriel!"

"Shh. It's all good. He's a strong one, our boy."

My heart soared at the confirmation he was still alive. "When can I see him?"

"Soon. He's asleep."

"I didn't ask when he could see me."

"Hey, doofus. Don't bite my head off. I have orders to keep you here in your bed."

I closed my eyes and let a wry smile run over my lips for a second. "Well, I'm afraid to tell you, but I'm not a pet dog." I sat up and narrowed my eyes, feeling the ecstatic lupine rush I remembered from so long ago. "I'm a damn wolf."

"Well, Mister Wolf, we have doctors here, too, you know. Not the high-falutin' fancy-pants Chicago surgeon kind, but they know their stuff."

I struggled to slide my damaged body off the bed, but Kiera pushed me back down. With far more ease than I'd have liked.

"You're killing me, here, cuz."

"Look, you're much better to stay here. My parents are in the waiting room, but the bad news is, so are yours."

"I can handle them."

"Ethan, there's more. Those guys?"

"The bears?"

"Uh-huh. We ran 'em down real quick. You shoulda seen my mom in full flight. Anyway, turns out those big idiots were nothing more than mercenary bullies. Took my dad all of ten seconds to get them talking once they shifted back." She chuckled without any humor. "One of them was real sorry. He had a stick in his ear when he shifted. Poor bastard will never hear on that side again."

I squeezed the blankets in my fists. "Nothing they said is of any interest to me. They touched my mate. And they were about to..." I swallowed my mounting fury as I remembered the scene.

Gabriel, naked and wounded.

That big fucking brute with his meaty hands on his tight, scrumptious ass.

"Those opportunistic pricks."

"See, that's the thing." Kiera walked over to the door of the ward, as if getting out of my reach. And maybe blocking my exit. "Like I said, they were mercenaries. It wasn't random. They were hired."

***

The Larsons and the Roddicks all looked up in shock as I limped into the waiting room, fresh blood seeping from the puncture wounds of the IV line I'd torn out.

"You two." I lined my parents up in my sights. "You tell me now. The truth."

Hugh stood and folded his arms. "The truth about what, son?"

"You're behind this? You tried to have

my mate killed?"

Olga Roddick scoffed and turned back to the magazine on her lap. "Please, son. You're being so dramatic." She flipped a couple of pages.

Hugh stepped in again. "We only told them to scare him off."

"So, the rape and murder which I only just managed to prevent? What, that was their bonus?"

Olga sighed. "That's what happens when you send a bear to do a wolf's job..." She stood, finally, and walked toward me, arms outspread. "We only want what's best. Now, let's just put this all behind us, son."

In my peripheral vision, Ethan saw Kiera walk over to the waiting room entrance to intercept the two men who were about to enter.

"Oh, I agree on one count, you cold-hearted bitch. This is all behind us now. You have your world, and I have mine. Let's make sure the two never mix again. I know how you feel about keeping things pure, after all."

"Son, you don't mean that. Come meet with Anthea. Properly this time."

I spat my voice out through gritted teeth. "My final reminder, Mrs Roddick. You do not get to call me son. Not now. Not ever. Now, rather than having me meet Anthea, I think you should turn around and meet these two gentlemen."

She spun instantly, almost running into the uniformed police officers who'd crept up behind her as only shifters can.

Olga turned back to face me. For a moment, she stood before me, unmoving. The whole waiting room fell silent. Then, for the first time I could recall, I saw tears in my mother's eyes.

"This is so typical of you, you stupid human-lover. We had a new mate for you. The right kind. Wolf."

"My mate is waiting for me down that corridor."

"He'll never be wolf."

I crossed my arms, and let my mouth curl up into a satisfied smile. "Oh, but I told you before... he already is." I snapped my teeth together to ram home the truth.

Olga's face drained of color as she processed that little reminder. She narrowed her eyes in rage for a moment, and then brought herself back under control.

"Well, I knew it would end badly with you, Ethan. I always wanted a daughter, anyway."

"Hey, I fuck men. Isn't that close enough?" The rush I got from being so damn dismissive was almost as heady as anything I felt with Gabriel.

Almost.

Olga spun away, as if in shame. Whether it was over her own actions, or over the actions of her flesh and blood, wasn't clear. And to me, it mattered less than a dead mosquito.

With my parents gone, my anger fell away, too. All I felt was weak. I turned as freely as I could and reached out for Kiera. Bernard Larson stepped in on the other side and together they supported me.

"Take me to him, please?"

Bernard shook his head. "Son, you need medical attention."

"Just for a minute. I know he's alive.

Even if Kiera hadn't told me, I'd know. I can feel it. But I need to see him for myself."

CHAPTER THIRTY-THREE

Gabriel

TWO DAYS HAD passed since the attack. At least, that's what they'd told me. And I hadn't seen Ethan once in that time. When I'd first awoken, my immediate thought was that maybe he didn't make it, but before that idea could even gather speed, my wolf stepped in. I could feel the truth, without being told. Ethan was alive.

And even more importantly, he was close.

My consciousness was still as random as hell. I faded in and out for another day or so.

When the darkness inside my head finally cleared, I struggled to sit up, to look around me. Before I could even open my eyes, strong hands gripped mine. At the moment of skin-to-skin contact, I knew for certain it was Ethan.

"Hey, butt-face."

"Little one. Welcome back."

Gradually, I managed to focus on those silver eyes of his, and a fresh burst of heat ran through my body. "Shouldn't you be in bed, too?"

"Hey, at least buy me a drink first."

My laughter soon turned to coughing. "Don't do that to me, asshole. You know what I meant." I pointed at the bandaging on his belly.

"I know, but by your side is the only place I want to be, lover." He pushed his point home by raising my hand to his lips for the softest of kisses.

I vaguely remembered being pissed at him. I even remembered what caused it. None of that mattered anymore.

I pressed my hand gently to his cheek, and soaked up the look of peace that crossed his face. "They tell me I probably would've died if... if I'd still been human."

Ethan bowed his head, as if picturing exactly that. "Probably."

"So, do I get to know what it was all for? Why we were almost killed?"

Ethan sighed heavily. "You won't like it."

"Hey, fangs and claws may break my jaws, but words will never hurt me." I caught the look in Ethan's eyes and felt my insides ice up. "What? Who were those guys?"

Ethan shook his head. "They were just guys. A couple of rogues, doing what they were paid for. They're locked up now and probably will be for a while."

Clear thinking was still difficult, and I rubbed my fingers on the back of Ethan's hand while I formed the words. "You know, butt-face, I'm gonna get the rest of the info out of you one way or another. I always do. You might as well just tell me."

He lowered his gaze, studying my fingers, my arm. Apparently, anything other than looking me in the face.

"It was my parents. You didn't fit into their planning." He zeroed back in on my eyes. "But I think you probably knew that already."

I did, but even so, it still cut like crazy. To think anyone could be so cold, and so out of touch with their own child, went against every instinct I had ever felt. If we were ever lucky enough to adopt kids, I'd just have to follow the lessons of my own family. Except the part about being killed when they were young.

Before they died, my parents had been hard when it came to discipline, but they'd never once turned me away from any of my dreams. All they ever demanded was that I make it count, or else give it up. I realized only now that I'd failed at that before Ethan came into my life.

And that he was exactly what I needed to live my life completely fulfilled.

Ethan sounded close to tears when he spoke again. "I mean, they claim it was a scare tactic. That the bears simply didn't know when to stop." He swallowed before continuing. "But to think my own flesh and blood would go so far to get you out of my life is beyond contemptible. I'm so sorry, little one."

"Hey. You don't apologize for what anyone else did." I fought against the pain and fatigue, getting myself upright and wrapping my arms around Ethan's neck. "Don't forget. You saved me, butt-face."

"God, you saved me so much more, Gabe. And not just from the bears." He kissed my shoulder and grasped my hand, placing it to the center of his chest. "You made me whole, little one. And I can't wait to spend the rest of my life with you."

My belly tingled at the thought, and I knew it was more than simple excitement.

"And there's someone else who can't wait to sink his teeth into you, too."

He released me and looked deep into my eyes. "You can feel your wolf?"

"Uh-huh."

Ethan placed his hand on my chest, mirroring what he'd done with my own hand. "I can't wait to meet him."

"You're not scared? You know, that you'll get stuck with four legs instead of two?"

His smile bloomed inside me. "Nothing scares me when I'm with you, little one." He cupped my head in his hands and kissed me on the nose. "Except the thought of losing you."

"As soon as we're out of here, we're taking this thing to the next level, Ethan."

"Oh? And what level is that?"

"The rest of our lives. As man and...

wolf."

THE END

Thank you for reading the Gray Vale Pack series. I hope you enjoyed these romantic shifter tales, and who knows, perhaps in the future we will see more of the growly men of Gray Vale and Stoke Ridge in the other delicious paranormal romance stories my mind is sure to deliver.

In the meantime, if you enjoyed this book, please do me a favor and leave me a review. I do read them, and even a few positive words will help me in crafting more of the books my readers love.

Thank you!

~Evie Riley

OTHER BOOKS BY EVIE

Federal Protection Agency

Mason
Rafe
Ryzen
Cooper
Noah
Damien
Sebastian
Gabe
Logan

Ruthless Empire

Courting Danger
Chasing Danger
Kissing Danger

Smokejumpers

Hawke
Cyrus
Jase
Gage
Jackson
Xavier

Jasper Springs
Cade
Dawson
Drew
Grayson
Riley
Mitch

From The Edge
Shattered
Runaway
Jaded
Rescue
Hidden
Tormented

Gray Vale Pack
His Fated Mate
His Wounded Warrior
His Healing Heart

ABOUT THE AUTHOR

Evie Riley is a prolific, neurodivergent author known for her captivating MM romance novels. She has gained a significant following and topped the LGBT+ action and adventure bestseller charts with her series.

Evie's writing style often explores dark and gritty themes where her men must overcome difficult obstacles in their search for love, but she has also ventured into sweeter small-town romances, incorporating tropes like enemies-to-lovers, friends-to-lovers, age-gap, and forced proximity. She is known for crafting engaging romantic suspense novels and has a knack for creating interconnected series worlds that keep readers invested.

EVIE RILEY

Interestingly, Ms. Riley has hinted at exploring new genres, such as Alien Omegaverse Romance, in the future.

Outside of writing, she enjoys spending time at the beach and has a quirky personality, described by her partner as ranging from cute to deadly, depending on her blood-chocolate levels.

Evie spends her nights writing bad boys in love, and her days wrangling the sweet boys she loves.

www.ingramcontent.com/pod-product-compliance
Lightning Source LLC
Chambersburg PA
CBHW061054210726
48294CB00001B/138